I0646617

the
unsafe asylum

Stories of
Partition and
Madness

Anirudh Kala

SPEAKING
TIGER

SPEAKING TIGER PUBLISHING PVT. LTD
4281/4 Ansari Road, Daryaganj,
New Delhi – 110002, India

First published in India in paperback by Speaking Tiger 2018

ISBN: 978-93-87693-27-2
eISBN: 978-93-87693-26-5

10 9 8 7 6 5 4 3 2 1

Typeset in Adobe Caslon Pro by Jojy Philip
Printed at Shree Maitrey Printech Pvt. Ltd., Noida

In 'The Mad Prophesier' pp. 126–9 were previously published
as the short story 'Mr Haq' in Muse India

Anirudh Kala lives in Ludhiana and is a psychiatrist. His interests include studying the lasting effects of Partition in both India and Pakistan. He has been instrumental in cross-border exchanges between the two countries among mental health professionals and many of his stories result from his own visits to mental health institutes in Pakistan. He has published several short stories. He likes Urdu poetry, hiking and semi-classical Indian music.

*This book is dedicated to the memory of
my friend and colleague, Dr Haroon Rashid Chaudhry,
Executive Director of Fountainhouse, Lahore.*

CONTENTS

NO FORGIVENESS NECESSARY

June, 1947

Mental Hospital, Lahore

As he passed through the fortress-like gates of the Mental Hospital on his wobbly bicycle, the drizzle became a downpour and all the lights went off. It was one of those abrupt violent showers which sometimes follow a dust storm during peak summer in Punjab. Dr Iqbal Junaid Hussain was on night duty. He pulled off his sodden skullcap and thrust it into a pocket. Walking with the cycle now, he buttoned the raincoat up till the chin, over his flowing beard, and then bent down to pull off the shiny metal clasps that kept his sodden pyjamas from getting caught in the bicycle chain. Iqbal was a religious man, and preferred to wear pyjamas which were convenient for prostrating during namaaz.

A hundred and seventy acres lay before him, eerily silent, and shrouded in complete darkness. Shivering, Iqbal wondered if anybody could have guessed that the campus housed more than twelve hundred seriously disturbed mentally ill patients. His shivers were not because of the cold. As a matter of fact, it was rather warm, with heat seeping out of the scorching earth as it drizzled. Iqbal shuddered again, recollecting the bedlam he'd witnessed that evening on his way here.

As he pushed his cycle against the lashing rain, a streak of lightning lit up the ground and he could see the gravel path fork left, towards his office. The flower beds on both sides were brimming with water and his black oxfords were now covered with mud. As if on cue, a faint glimmer of torchlight, dimmed by sheets of rain started moving towards him and a raucous 'Salaam-alekum!' followed by a hesitant 'Sat-sriakal' greeted him.

Fattu and Rulda were huddled together under a ragged umbrella. They both wore outsized uniforms with tall grey-and-black stripes which made them look more like prisoners-of-war than patients in a hospital. The uniforms, in fact, happened to be war surplus, like many things in the hospital. But technically, the two men who wore them were no longer patients. Both had been discharged from the hospital a month ago, within a few days of each other. Iqbal had sent two pale yellow half-anna postcards carrying the haughty image of King George VI, one to Rulda Singh's village near Rawalpindi, and the other to Fateh Mohammed's village beyond Hoshiarpur.

'Dear Sir,' he had written in his flowing handwriting, using a new metal nib and the shiny black ink for the special occasion, 'I am very happy to inform you that your young ward has recovered to such an extent that he is fit to go home. He has been discharged by the Visitors' Board and now you are requested to come and receive custody of him on any working day between 9 a.m. and 2 p.m., after signing the required papers. Please note that as per the hospital policy, a discharged patient can be handed over only to a near relative. You are also requested to bring your ration card for purposes of identification.' Feeling the happiness that a messenger of glad tidings is entitled to, he had waited along with the boys for weeks, but no one had come.

Iqbal could easily understand that the two families, finding themselves on the wrong sides of a looming, even if so far tentative, border between India and Pakistan, would have had more compelling issues of life, death, home and hearth on their minds than collecting a 'kamla' family member from the hospital, even if he had partly recovered. They might even have speculated amongst themselves that a mental hospital was a safer place than the world outside in that summer of 1947. On that particular rainy evening, Iqbal was in absolute agreement with that point of view.

When it became clear that no one was coming for them, he did not bother to follow the tortuous rigmarole of re-admitting Rulda and Fattu under the Indian Lunacy Act—taking them to a magistrate, cooking up signs of 'lunacy' which did not exist and answering awkward questions about why they had been discharged in the first place. He simply asked them to sleep on the wooden benches outside his office, take their medicines from the pharmacy and eat in the mess. In return, they were supposed to make themselves generally useful to the staff.

Whenever the night driver was on leave, which was often during those troubled times, Rulda drove the ramshackle ambulance for Iqbal's night rounds. This relict of the war was the only motorized vehicle that the hospital had. It needed a stiff crank with the handle to start it and had the words, 'War Organization of the British Red Cross Society' painted on both its olive-green sides.

Rulda drove the ambulance with Iqbal sitting in front and Fattu at the back. The paths connecting the wards were all a watery slush. Wheels skidded at the turns, but Rulda seemed to divine each curve in the road well in advance, even in the dark. The headlights had been dim for days, as the alternator needed repairs. Having lived there for three years, Rulda Singh and Fateh Mohammed knew the land around the mental hospital like the backs of their young, gnarled hands, even on those dark nights when there was neither moonlight nor electricity. The buildings were scattered without any particular architectural logic across the expanse of farmland, dignified by the title of campus— twelve general wards, the insulin coma unit, the ECT unit, the administrative block, tube wells, several sheds, workshops and kitchen blocks with chimneys belching smoke throughout the day. A meandering irrigation waterway drawn from a canal flowed serenely along the road outside the hospital. In no time, they had deposited him at his office, where someone had thoughtfully left a lantern burning in the window.

Dr Iqbal Hussain was one of the two Deputy Medical Superintendents at the hospital. Despite having been in the job longer, he was junior in rank because his colleague, Dr Satinder Sharma, was a regular medical graduate. Iqbal was a 'licentiate', with a shorter three-year diploma, rather than a five-year degree course. 'Let us do it step by step,' his father, a pharmacist attached to a popular practice, had tried to explain. 'I am a doctor's assistant; you will be a doctor, and your son a proper specialist. Besides, this course is all I can afford.'

Dr David Patchett, the medical superintendent, perceived Iqbal to be 'methodical, dependable and predictable, but not the sharpest tool in the shed', according to his latest annual confidential report. Sharma's report, in contrast, contained words like 'brilliant' and 'quirky'. Any work that required time and diligence or involved crunching figures was left by the British psychiatrist for Iqbal to complete. His junior status as a 'diploma doctor' was also the reason that the lion's share of night duties fell to him, a fact lamented on a daily basis by his wife, Rashida.

Iqbal brought the lantern to the table to read the day report left for him by his senior. The superintendent had to send reports to the state government about everything from the cost of meat and vegetables consumed per patient per month, to the expenditure per year on laundering hospital uniforms. The medical superintendent prided himself on being a psychiatrist and not an administrator, and when he left for the day, he sent all such papers to Iqbal's table. Now, with Dr Patchett feverishly busy with his impending return to London for good, more and more such work was being left on Iqbal's desk.

Squinting behind his glasses to compensate for the dim, smoky light, Iqbal skimmed over the three-page day report. It seemed to have been a routine day at the hospital which, to Iqbal, after what he had been through in the city, was in itself a miracle. One hundred and fifty-two patients had been seen in the out-patient department and two fresh cases had been admitted.

As he pushed away the report, Iqbal spotted a slim file lying on the table. It had a fresh cover held in place with a coarse bright-red flap and a neatly tied white cord. The thin file was like a newborn child. Iqbal could not contain his curiosity. He slid the day report into a drawer, pulled the knot open and impatiently flipped open the cover without waiting for the electricity to return. He tried to raise the wick of the lantern, but only managed to get dark smoke to billow out of the holes at the top, filling the room with the sharp smell of kerosene. He quickly rolled down the wick by rotating the loop at its base, and tried to make do with the little light available. There was not much to read anyway. A bland three-line note written in blue ink with a familiar flair, requested 'Dr Iqbal Junaid Hussain, Deputy Medical Superintendent, Grade-II, to prepare a list of names and addresses of all Hindu and Sikh patients admitted at MHL at the earliest.'

His mind refused to focus and read further. Iqbal tried to reason with himself. He was simply being asked to prepare a run-of-the-mill report. The hospital records routinely tabulated the numbers of admitted patients according to religion. In fact, Iqbal knew that 678 of the 1,267 patients there that night were Hindus and Sikhs. They were habitually clubbed together for all practical purposes because of their shared ethnicity, and also sometimes collectively categorized as Hindus, much to the consternation of the Sikhs. Of the remaining 589, 560 were Muslim, twenty were Christian and nine, Parsi. There was no reason to brace himself. So why was he feeling so alarmed?

Then, in a moment of epiphany, Iqbal realized what was wrong with the note. In his eleven years of writing reports and preparing neat tables for his seniors, he had only dealt with numbers. For the first time, he was being asked to compile a list of the names and addresses of patients from specific religions.

His apprehension was backed by the next line he read: 'This is for the purpose of their possible deportation to India after the Partition of the country which appears to be imminent. We must not be found unprepared at our end, to make place for Muslim patients who would be coming from mental hospitals on the Indian side.'

Iqbal was not a qualified psychiatrist and lacked the skill of professional detachment, which can be relative at best. Over the years, he had spent long hours with the patients, feeling their moods, cringing at their nightmares, getting exasperated over good-for-nothing fathers, truant mothers, groping uncles, unfaithful wives and fist-happy husbands. Iqbal's patients were his only social life and he trusted their accounts implicitly. He was baffled at the possibility that half of them would just be taken away, even if on a promise of replacement. His brain conjured up images of 678 of his patients—240 of whom were women—wearing grey hospital uniforms with numbers stamped on their backs, being goaded by bearded, gun-toting guards into dark train coaches for the thirty-mile journey to Amritsar.

He wondered if somewhere across the dark expanse of the country that night, somebody on the 'other side' also had been asked to prepare a similar list of Muslim patients destined to be railroaded in the opposite direction.

His mind went back to that afternoon at his house. Rashida, his second wife, had been patting two-month-old Asif to sleep with one hand, and holding an English newspaper with the other, trying to read while lying in bed. She was an English teacher at the government school for girls, which was almost next door. Iqbal had been surprised that the newspaper was still delivered; milk no longer was, and the streets had been empty of vendors for days.

Reading aloud, she'd informed Iqbal that the blaze of anarchy in the city was likely to rage that day too. Waving the newspaper, she reminded him that the decision to split the country had been confirmed. '*A Partition Council has already begun the humongous task*', she'd read from that day's editorial, '*of dividing the country and its sprawling assets into two; everything from land and money in the Treasury, to men in army, horses in stables, the police, their weaponry, railway coaches and engines, tables and chairs, registers, heaps and*

*heaps of files and so on. All those in government service have
been asked to choose which future country they would want to
serve, India or Pakistan.'*

'Where are my socks Rashida, the blue ones?' Iqbal had
interrupted. 'And I know all about that. Wasn't I asked? I
already ticked Pakistan on the pro-forma.'

'Since when have you started fussing over the colour of
your socks? Is there a new nurse on night duty?' she'd teased
and slipped in her pet grouse, 'You have been sleeping since
morning, Dr Owl. I hardly get to talk to you. And I read
all this because I am worried for us. In a riot anybody can
get killed. When there is a fire, it spreads and fire does not
know a Hindu from Muslim. Does it?' With that she went
back to her editorial. *'Killings and rioting in Punjab started
in March because people on the "wrong side" of the future border
are sitting ducks for religious zealots-turned-goons and goons-
turned-religious zealots. The District Magistrate of Lahore,
Mr Eustace, said the other day that Muslim rowdies of Lahore
had received from their counterparts in Amritsar, a packet of
henna and glass bangles ridiculing their manliness. The next
day, the sprawling Hindu-Sikh mohalla of Shah Aalmi was
burnt to ashes. The smoke could be seen for three days from as
far as Ferozewala across the Raavi.'*

Rashida, with her fetish of poring over every newspaper
that came her way, was far more aware of the dire realities
of Punjab that fateful summer than her husband. Iqbal's
main preoccupations—other than his work—were prayer,
five times a day, and reading the authoritative Bleuler's

Textbook of Psychiatry (in his scheme of things it ranked lower only to the Koran) whenever and wherever he could. And, of course, listening to All India Radio, Lahore, which, being government-run, purveyed staid and conservative commentaries on the otherwise anarchic events. His main ambition was to qualify as a psychiatrist and for that he had to first pass an examination to get into Maudsley Hospital in London, the Mecca of Psychiatry in those days. The other, of course, was to travel to the real Mecca, for the pilgrimage, as soon he could afford it.

Having cast aside the newspaper, Rashida was now fully on her own, 'Do you know that the man Radcliffe, who is already in Delhi drawing the boundary line, came to India for the first time just last week? And do you know what his profession is?' She paused, ratcheting up the suspense. Iqbal shook his head.

'He is a lawyer! A lawyer for God's sake, and here he is, etching a boundary spanning two thousand miles of hills, plains, deserts and marshes. He is going to complete the job in a month! Using shoddy maps and the wrong census figures. And it is being done in secrecy. You see, England has no money after the war and they have no patience either for doing things properly. They want to cut and run. Even Churchill has called it "a shameful flight and a hurried scuttle." Mountbatten must have seen the riots coming— everybody else did—and still did not care. It is as though he wants to say: "You wanted freedom, no? Here, enjoy!"'

'The worry is making you crazy, woman. You should

pray regularly like I do. I tell you, it helps. And we are going to be alright. Have trust in Allah.'

Iqbal had not wanted to miss his night duty. He told Rashida that he had never taken leave in eleven years except when Hamida, his first wife, had died of smallpox ten years ago. Rashida had, of course, heard this many times before. She had replied caustically, 'Heavens will not fall if the crazies in the mental hospital don't have a doctor for one night. In any case they don't have a real illness. And there are nurses and orderlies.'

'Can't you see,' she'd added 'you have not been put on a single day duty since this started?' Both her hands were free now that Asif was asleep, and while saying 'this', she made a wide generous sweep, taking in the whole city.

Iqbal had reasoned, passing his fingers through his flowing beard, 'Lahore has been emptied of half its Hindus and Sikhs, and the other half would be too scared for their own lives to harm someone so obviously a Muslim.'

'If you have to go, then go nice and early. You do nothing at home anyway except sleep; might as well reach before dark,' Rashida had urged, mixing her favourite blend of tender and abrasive concern, her anxiety showing through clearly.

Just then, the dust storm presaging the rain had raged through and the house was filled with wind and dust. As the two ran from one window to another, Asif had started bawling. It was another hour before the weather settled down. By the time Iqbal had left home after an early dinner, it was already close to seven. He'd clamped his folded raincoat and the psychiatry textbook in a plastic cover to the cycle carrier and set off.

~

As he turned into Gawal Mandi from the Lohari Gate road, the market's stillness hit Iqbal like a wallop. He peered at his watch, balancing the cycle with one hand. It was only five minutes after seven. In the light of the setting sun the silent market lay before him like a dead person. Iqbal was so taken aback that he dismounted from his cycle as if in awe of the deathly quiet.

The road had never looked so wide. Not one shop was open and there was not a man in sight. The normally frenetic tonga stand at the corner of the square was completely empty, its moss-lined water trough the only sign of horse or human life. A stray dog was feebly trying to get through the broken window of a shop. The huge signboard, announcing 'Manchanda Cakes and Pastries, Lahore and Simla' hung down precariously from a single bolt, dividing the wide shopfront into two. Iqbal and Rashida had come here just two weeks ago, the day he had got his salary, dodging the bustle and smells of the market. A narrow staircase next to the shop led up to the offices of the Empire of India Assurance Company. Every three months, Iqbal climbed these stairs to deposit the premium for his life insurance policy.

The houses beyond the main crossing looked equally desolate, with not a door or window open. As he turned onto McLeod Road, there was a faint call of 'Nara-etakbeer' followed by a full-throated 'Allah-o-Akbar', somewhere in the direction of where he'd come from. That quickly put paid to the idea which he was reluctantly entertaining; of going back to Rashida and telling her that she was right. He cycled on, uneasily, through the silent and deserted husk of the neighbourhood.

Then, abruptly, there was a long row of houses, one after the other, completely charred. Looking at the smouldering shells in horror, Iqbal realized that he'd admired the green curtains with huge purple flowers in one of these houses while returning from work that very morning.

An easterly breeze brought dense smoke and a sickly smell. Fighting cough and nausea, Iqbal started cycling faster. Then, suddenly, the houses were intact again, though most were marked—branded with over-sized crosses in white paint—as Hindu and Sikh houses. A local scouting party had done its work well for the convenience of the murderous gang coming from another part of the city. Would they also be lifeless shells a couple of hours later in the night? As this thought crossed his mind, Iqbal realized what had been nagging him since he had left home: he had not seen a single policeman.

The bicycle chain creaked shrilly, slicing through the silence, as he pushed the paddles hard to turn into Lawrence Road. He almost fell down as he swerved to avoid the two tongas lying upturned in the middle of the road, just past the corner. The colourful awnings were crushed under the weight of the tongas, the wheels turned helplessly skywards. Their horses were nowhere to be seen. The front wheel of his cycle touched what seemed to be a charred log at first. Iqbal recoiled from the way it yielded. The smell of kerosene hung heavy in the air, and if Iqbal had been in any state to count, he would have counted seven burnt bodies lying across the road, strewn between the jumble of tongas and empty steel trunks with gaping lids. From the molten red and green glass around their wrists, two had probably been women. Shivering and retching, he turned back and ran, his heart pounding. He was not sure later whether he actually saw or just imagined in his panicked state of mind, a red sari trailing around the corner of the narrow lane.

Running breathlessly alongside his cycle, he turned left and, within minutes, found himself in a surprisingly mundane shopping area. Tremulous and wheezing, he rested the cycle against a wall and sat on the wooden plank set before the nearest shopfront. As his breathing became less laboured, he looked around and realized that he was in Mozang, a staunchly Muslim neighbourhood. Many shops were open, most with doors tentatively half-ajar.

Just when he thought he could resume his ride to the hospital, Iqbal heard the sputtering of a motorcycle. A hefty Sikh with a flowing beard drove into view, riding a Royal Enfield. He was stopped at the meat shop at the corner, where a green banner with a crescent moon stretched above the carcasses. Iqbal knew that there was a popular mosque inside the lane. A group of men in kurtas and salwars, who had been hanging around after the maghrib prayer, surrounded the motorcycle. As the circle tightened, the Sikh raised his Webley revolver with a brisk practised movement, and fired into the air with a straight arm. The gaggle of men scattered away into the lane but regrouped almost immediately. By then, he had roared away.

Before the crowd could gather itself to pursue him, an old Sikh came into view from another lane, walking slowly. Carpentry tools stuck out of the cloth bag he carried on his back. Conspicuous and exposed, he paused under the eyes of the men. One of them had snatched up a cleaver from the meat shop. As he sensed the menace in their posture, he turned and ran. Within seconds, the mob was pursuing him like a pack of hounds. A young man with a white cap who had been sitting at the corner and not taking part in the proceedings so far, stretched out his foot as the carpenter passed him. Even before the old Sikh fell, the mob was upon him.

Nobody noticed a middle-aged bearded man sitting on his haunches in front of an open drain, retching his guts out.

The marketplace was full of swirling clouds of dust. The street had emptied suddenly. It was surreal, the stage of a fast-moving macabre play emptying itself between acts. Iqbal was left alone, sitting on the ground, his head in his hands. Ten feet away, the headless body of the old carpenter lay with his tools and lunch box scattered around him.

As the storm intensified, a garish pink signboard, unhinged from somewhere, fell into the square with a loud crash. Iqbal looked at it. With a gaudy sketch of a rather fetching middle-aged woman, the hoarding promised a concert of scintillating qawwalis by Jammeela Bai Ambale-wali, at the Jubilee Town Hall on Saturday evening.

~

Iqbal tried to pull down the enamel lampshade hanging from the office roof for better light, but the shade was too hot to touch. He peered at the slanting handwriting of his superior once again, pulled out a fresh register from a drawer, and started to copy down in neat columns, the names, fathers' (or husbands') names and the addresses of the 678 Hindu and Sikh patients admitted at Mental Hospital Lahore, for possible deportation.

~

At one, while rain still pitter-pattered on the slanting roof of the office, there were heavy footfalls in the corridor. The gateman, Dilshad Khan, a Pathan, came in, his shirt and salwar drenched despite the umbrella from the long walk from the hospital gate. It seemed that a Sikh and a Hindu family were at the gate with their five children, asking for shelter till the morning. 'Their homes are burnt and streets dangerous Sahibji. And it is raining.' Dilshad Khan was pleading as much as reporting.

Iqbal nodded. 'Let them stay in the waiting hall. And wake up Afzal in the kitchen; they'll need some food and milk.'

A little later, still hard at work, Iqbal heard Fattu and

Rulda talking through the open window, as they sat on the bench outside his office.

'Have the outsiders gone mad?' Rulda wanted to know.

Fattu chuckled, 'Yes, they have.'

'You really think so?' Rulda's amusement and interest was clear.

'We are at least predictable!' said Fattu condescendingly.

'Not always.' Rulda was a fair man.

'Well, we are predictably unpredictable. Outsiders are unpredictably unpredictable. That makes us more predictable. They should be inside and us outside.'

'But they are so many. All of them cannot fit in here,' Rulda objected to the logistics of the proposition. 'So many people cannot be mad.'

'Why?' Fattu wanted to know, swatting a mosquito on his arm.

'The majority has to be sane,' Rulda did not sound fully convinced himself.

'Why?' Fattu persisted monotonously.

'Because if most people were insane, the world would come crashing down.' Rulda thought that it was a rather good argument.

'Maybe it is crashing down as we speak.' Fattu observed. He liked to needle Rulda during their midnight debates. Now he took the attack to Rulda. 'You, Non-Muslim mental patient! You will be deported to Hindustan with all the other Hindu and Sikh kaffirs.' Iqbal guessed correctly that they had overheard the nurses talking during the day.

One of the many disadvantages of perpetual night duty was that one missed out on hospital gossip.

Rulda objected, 'My house is here, near Rawalpindi and yours near Hoshiarpur in Hindustan.'

'Don't worry! They will shift the houses too. They will send your house there and bring mine here. Outside people are very smart.' An infant began to wail distantly from the waiting hall.

'Ghanta, smart!' But Rulda seemed to be convinced by Fattu's argument. He spat out the tobacco that he had been carrying under his cheek with full force, 'They are killing people faster than you can kill mosquitoes. They need electric shocks.' Then his pragmatic side took over, 'But all of Lahore? We do not have that much electricity.'

Fattu agreed. There was a pause. Then. 'You know the big sign over the gate which reads Mental Hospital, Lahore? We should take it down and put it up inside, so that everybody is clear which side of the gate is the actual mental hospital.'

Iqbal smiled and pushed the register and file away to get up for his night rounds.

~

It was nearly four by the time Iqbal returned to his office and asked Fattu to fetch tea from the kitchen. When he looked out of the window an hour and a half later, the rain had stopped. He switched off the light. By seven, he had transferred more than a hundred entries from the register to the new file, which was now eight pages thick.

He decided to take the papers home to complete the task during the day, despite Rashida's inevitable protests.

At a quarter to eight, Iqbal put on his socks, scraped the caked mud off his shoes and tied up the laces. Having made a neat packet of the raincoat, the *Textbook of Psychiatry*, the register and the new file, he fixed it securely to the cycle carrier. He clamped his pyjamas at the calves with the steel clasps, put on his skullcap and, at eight exactly, cycled out of the gate, answering Dilshad's rather smart ex-army salute with a cursory wave of his hand.

As Iqbal turned his cycle onto the Jail Road, he felt a sense of calm in the bright air around him, as if after the previous day's convulsions, the city had woken up fresh and at peace. The roar of a motorcycle came towards him rapidly and then stopped. As he drew his cycle to a halt, Iqbal vaguely remembered that he had seen the tall Sikh in Army fatigues somewhere. His gaze was mesmerized by the glint of sunshine on the shiny black surface of the revolver; he didn't register the sound of the single shot that killed him.

~

The motorcycle stopped a mile away. Its driver, who had promised himself ten that night, threw the gun away listlessly and, sitting on the berm, started sobbing like a child.

* * *

December 1979

Phagwara, Indian Punjab

The air-conditioned bus from Amritsar to Delhi stopped for an unscheduled halt on the Grand Trunk Road in front of some makeshift shops selling fruit juice. A tall, handsome man wearing a cotswool shirt, just appropriate for the early December weather, was the only passenger who got down. The man looked around to get his bearings, then walked purposefully across the road, with long, eager steps. He seemed to know the way rather well for a newcomer.

The other side of the highway was lined with car-repair workshops. All of these, he had been told, catered exclusively to imported cars. Many Punjabis, who had worked abroad and had money to spare, had brought along a Mercedes or a BMW, since they were exempt from paying the exorbitant import duty on cars. Since imported cars were otherwise not sold in the country, very few mechanics were familiar with the innards of these. The only workshops which could repair these cherished machines in the whole of the northern region were here, on one side of the busy highway in this dusty town. People were known to drive or tow their cars from as far as Simla and stay in a hotel in Ludhiana or Jalandhar while their Precious was being serviced. Most of the cars lined up in front of the workshops were Mercedes, in various stages of repair. But the man, being a car buff, could easily spot a deep yellow Ford Mustang with the doors ajar, an electric blue BMW coupe resting on supports, followed by the shell of a grand, silver-grey convertible Rolls Royce Corniche, stripped of its seats and with the steering panel jutting straight up from the floor.

Several people were at work on the cars, but the man from the bus did not ask for any directions. He chose to methodically scan the signboards of the workshops, starting from one end of the market, and soon found what he was looking for. A man as tall as himself, but much older, was bent under the wide hood of a cherry red Chevrolet Corvair; the visitor could see just his back and the edge of his turban. His baggy trousers were held up with a pair of leather suspenders worn over a ribbed vest. The visitor looked up again at the signboard saying 'Lahore Mercedes Centre' for confirmation. He cleared his throat and politely said, 'Excuse me, sir' to the older man, who straightened himself slowly with some effort. Turning, he saw a dapper young man in brown moccasins, beige jeans and a checked shirt, an obvious client. But the eyes were vaguely familiar. The young man looked at the Sikh car mechanic closely, at his cotton vest, the leather suspenders, the greying eyebrows, placed wide apart, and at the prominent mole above the left eye.

'Mr Ramneek Singh?' the stranger asked, putting his right hand in his jeans pocket, as if to take out something.

The car mechanic, quite perplexed, nodded.

'Sir, you dropped this. It was a long time ago. I have come to return it.' The visitor produced a worn, olive-green booklet, which he opened at the second page to show a yellowed photograph of Havaldar Ramneek Singh as a young man in Army uniform. The picture was cracked at the edges. The booklet had a handwritten number and the unit address of the Bengal Engineer Group, Roorkee Cantonment, in bold type.

Ramneek Singh did not extend his hand to take the document. Instead he asked, 'Where did you find it?'

'I did not find it.'The young man replied in a matter-of-fact tone. He continued steadily, with his eyes on Ramneek Singh's face, 'My father, Dr Iqbal Junaid Hussain, was killed on the morning of 28th June, 1947 outside the Mental Hospital, Lahore. He had just finished his night duty. The hospital gateman collected his belongings from the road and gave them to my mother. It seems your identity card was one of the articles. I was two months old then. I was shown this when I grew up. This is the first time I have been able to come "this side". I thought I should return it to the rightful owner.'

Ramneek Singh now knew why the visitor's eyes were familiar. Feeling weak, he leaned against the fender of the car. 'You know my name. What is yours?'

'Asif. Dr Asif Junaid Hussain. I am a psychiatrist.'

In the last thirty-two years Ramneek Singh had lain awake many nights, trying to cauterize from his consciousness the memory of the morning Asif had so matter-of-factly conjured up. So far, Ramneek had been a fugitive only from himself. Now, two people knew. He himself, and this suave gentleman, an ambassador from his past. Ramneek Singh was not afraid. He also knew that no one had been punished for any of the million murders that happened that summer. The thought that had confused and tormented him for half his life was simple: 'the man who did "that" was me. But this is not who I am.'

Ramneek Singh was aware that the roadside was not the best place to carry on the conversation which might follow. He was finding it difficult to look the young man in the eye while talking, but he felt a flicker of curiosity. 'And who gave you this address?'

'Your army unit. A friend in India wrote to them giving your number and said that some old belongings had to be returned. They were very helpful. They wrote back to say that Subedar Major Ramneek Singh of the Bengal Engineers had been honourably discharged on attaining superannuation, and gave this address. I see that you are putting your technical experience to good use.'

Ramneek nodded, accepting the recital of facts. There was a short pause, curiously untroubled for both of them. He leaned over and unhooked his shirt, carefully hung up away from any machine oil stains, realizing that he was resigned to Asif's appearance in his workshop. In any case, Asif was from Pakistan, and hence a very special guest, howsoever awkward the circumstances. While buttoning the cuffs, he gestured, 'My house is just here.' Unhesitatingly, Asif followed him out of the workshop.

He escorted Asif into the narrow lane behind the parked Chevrolet and into the open door of a house behind the workshop. The lobby was dark and cool after the bright sun outside, but some light entered through a barred opening in the ceiling, much like in houses that Asif had seen in the old parts of Lahore. As his eyes adjusted, he saw two young boys with jooda topknots, playing brisk table tennis. A man as old as him, possibly Ramneek's son, was sitting at the dining table. He rose upon seeing a guest with his father, but did not speak. The two entered a sitting room dominated by the large logo of an army unit, fitted in a glass cover above the mantelpiece. The sofa set and cane couch lined the walls facing it.

Ramneek closed the door to muffle the clickety-clack of the game. As they sat, he spoke, mildly enough, for the challenging words: 'Did you come all the way just to return my old ID papers, which you very well know I do not need?'

'No, I did not come just for this. I have come to watch a cricket match, the one that Pakistan and India are playing in Delhi tomorrow. Since I was passing by, I thought I would return the papers too.'

Asif paused to stand and fold his hands in greeting to the lady who now came in, carrying a tray with two cups of tea. 'My wife,' Ramneek introduced her. 'Asif has come from Lahore.' On hearing the word 'Lahore', the old lady came up to Asif and passed a soft hand smelling faintly of mint over his face and then over his head, for which he had to bend. He looked at the vivacious eyes and the almost pretty face. The droop in the mouth on one side meant that she was recovering from a stroke. She picked up the tray and went out, closing the door softly behind her.

'She had paralysis. Her leg and arm are alright now but she cannot speak. Doctors say it will take time.' Ramneek Singh could not help talking about the medical issue bothering him, now that there was a doctor in the sitting room.

'I am sorry to hear this, but I am sure that her speech will come back. It mostly does,' Asif reassured him.

Nobody spoke for a long time.

Asif resumed the conversation from where it was interrupted, 'Now that I am here, I might as well ask, "why did you shoot my father?"'

Ramneek's mind was still full of the troubling details of his wife's illness; they scattered away like pigeons as Asif spoke. With a suddenly dry throat, he got up to take a glass of water from the table. 'How do you know it was me who killed your father? It could have been anybody. The roads were full of killers in those days.' Ramneek knew this was just a faint attempt at parrying the question.

'Then how come your identity card was found in my father's effects?' Asif asked gently.

'Maybe I knew your father? Maybe I gave it to him for safe-keeping?'

'Did you know my father, Dr Iqbal Junaid Hussain, Deputy Medical Superintendent at Mental Hospital, Lahore?'

In a fresh surge of shame, Ramneek realized that the man he had killed was a doctor. In the last six months after his wife's stroke, he had met many doctors and his dependence on them during this vulnerable period meant that he viewed them as larger than life.

Ramneek was quiet for what seemed to both a very long time. Then, in a very low voice, he said, 'No.'

After another silent pause, Ramneek lifted his head and spoke without trying to avoid Asif's eyes.

'Yes, I shot your father. But I do not know why....

'All I know is that when I came home that evening, after being in Roorkee for a month, my ten-year-old son was lying in the courtyard, dead and covered in stab wounds. He was my only child then. He had been playing cricket in the lane when a mob ransacked the neighbourhood. My wife, whom you just met, saw it happen.'

The conversation had shifted from Urdu to Punjabi at some point. He continued, 'I am not condoning anything. Thousands of people who had their families slaughtered in front of their eyes did not kill anybody in return. And thousands of people who killed had not lost anybody. Your father had done me no harm. This is the way it happened, and I am simply narrating it. It may not answer your question, though.

'Everything in my insides gave way. I took a revolver and bullets from my suitcase, and drove out on my motorcycle. I swore by my Guru that I would not return till I had killed ten Muslims. I was in the army, but in an engineering battalion. I had never been in a battle. I had never killed anybody.

'I drove around the city in the rain the whole night, but could not bring myself to kill anybody. I felt broken but not angry...certainly not angry at the people on the road. I did not even want to shoot the cocky young boy at the petrol pump who made fun of my turban and refused to refill the motorcycle. I only shot once...a mob had surrounded me in Mozang, and I shot in the air, to give myself time to get away. Eventually, I drove out of the city in rain and wind, without knowing where I was going and collapsed somewhere in the fields.

'When I got up it was daylight. I did not remember what had been happening to me. The last I remembered was that I had boarded a train from Meerut to go to Lahore. I did not know what I was doing in the fields with my motorcycle parked next to me. I asked a farmer for directions back to Lahore.

'To reach my home, I had to pass near the paagal-khana, The sun had come up quite high by then and was blinding my eyes, making me slow down. Something said by the farmer who had given me directions, came to my mind. He had said that I was lucky to be alive. Why had he said that?

'Then it all came back, like a huge black torrent, waves after waves of darkness and anguish. I remembered the stab wounds on Harman's tiny chest. I could not drive. The motorcycle stalled in the middle of the road.

'Just then, I saw a man with a skullcap and a beard coming on a cycle from the other side. He stopped because I was blocking the way, and looked up at me. He had eyes like yours...

'I shot him. I do not know why.'

With his feet pulled up on the sofa, Ramneek Singh put his head on his knees, strands of grey showing through the loosely tied turban. Crouching like a child, he started sobbing.

Asif sat quietly, looking at him without any expression. He was trying to muffle the sobs, but Asif did not try to stop him from crying, even when he thought that somebody outside the room might hear him. The irregular rattle of the table tennis match continued. Ramneek Singh cried for a long time, as if making up for the lost time, as if grieving in the same sob together for his son Harman and for Iqbal Junaid Hussain, whom he did not know.

No forgiveness was asked for and none granted.

~

Outside the room, the kids interrupted their game to touch Asif's feet in quick perfunctory gestures. After a brief, touch-and-go hug, scared that he might start crying in front of others, Ramneek let Asif go.

Aman, Ramneek's son, dropped Asif at the railway station in a limousine with only two seats and no doors. While waiting for the train, he asked Asif if he could suggest a good sedative for his father's nightmares, which no Indian doctor had been able to cure. Asif tore off a corner of *The Tribune* that he had bought for the journey and scribbled the name of the first sedative which came to his mind.

As they shook hands, Asif said to Aman, 'Your father is a good man. Take care of him.'

~

Back in his hotel room in Amritsar, he took out the entry ticket for next day's India-Pakistan cricket match in Delhi and tore it into four pieces. It had served its purpose of getting him the Indian visa, no easy feat for a person from

Pakistan otherwise. He would have to think of a reason for going back without seeing the match. The good old standby of 'mother's illness' would be acceptable to immigration officers at both sides of the Wagah border, he decided.

That reminded him that his mother had insisted, 'You must go to the Golden Temple in Amritsar, on your way back. It is like Mecca for the Sikhs.' Asif left the room reluctantly, to reach the gurudwara before dark. She had also wanted the sweet parsad distributed by the priest at the end of each service, as proof that he actually went. As the lift doors opened, he reminded himself to pray, while there, that Ramneek Singh slept well tonight. Submitted directly to the relevant God, he thought, the prayer was more likely to work. The liftboy wondered why the tall handsome man in the camel-coloured jacket suddenly chuckled loudly to himself.

BELLY BUTTON

Guru Nanak's birth anniversary is usually celebrated in November, two weeks after Diwali. Nankana Sahib, the guru's birthplace, like those of millions of Punjabis, has been left behind in Pakistan. The government of Pakistan issues visas, an otherwise scarce commodity for Sikh pilgrims, to visit the sacred site on his birthday.

That year, a potential delegate had fractured his ankle while trying to negotiate a sharp turn on his scooter. The delegation leader, Mohinder Singh, remembered that his son's colleague, one Dr Prakash Kohli, had wanted to visit Pakistan. That was how Prakash found himself on a marigold-decked bus, full of noisy Sikh pilgrims on their way to Pakistan from Amritsar. He was the only clean-shaven, bare-headed man on the trip.

Prakash was alone; his wife, Jasmeet, could not go since there had been just one place available. He tied a yellow bandana around his head and opened his passport to look again at the visa granting him five days, including both days of travel, in Pakistan. It permitted him to visit only Lahore and Nankana Sahib, specifying that cantonment areas were out of bounds. To ensure that the visa holder did not go astray, the passport had to be stamped every day at the nearest police station.

A middle-aged man wearing the standard blue turban of the Akali party was nervously passing his fingers through his greying beard; his face had been glued to the window pane since they had crossed the border into Pakistan. As the bus took a turn and started moving along a canal, he shouted, 'Look at that canal. It was exactly the same when I used to jump naked from the bridge.' Faces turned back to look at him and he sheepishly added, 'Well, I was just ten.' Prakash noted that his eyes were moist.

As they reached the city, everybody in the bus agreed that Lahore was much cleaner and better organized than Amritsar and, of course, far bigger. They were like an excited bunch of kids on a school trip. There were comments about traffic being more disciplined, cars fancier and buildings better kept.

There were three constructs being compared. The real brick-and-mortar Lahore they were passing through, the Lahore they had been carrying in their minds and the Indian cities they were coming from. The younger pilgrims had just their parents' reminiscences of Lahore to go by. The older ones had their eyes peeled for familiar landmarks. There was envy. Pakistan, the archetypal enemy, seemed to be a rather fancy country. But for many it was a bit of a let-down, since it was also so similar, 'Same to same,' complained the young Sikh couple behind him to each other, 'Only the signboards are in Urdu and men wear salwars.' The woman in front of Prakash nudged her companion, 'No burqa! Not one so far.' She sounded cheated.

The drive to Nankana Sahib took an hour and a half. A young girl across the aisle commented that the canal network which criss-crossed the landscape looked very much like the one on the other side. Prakash noticed how the meaning of the word 'other side' had reversed in the last two hours. The tall thin man in a tie and tweed jacket who was sitting next to him introduced himself as a soil scientist and explained that the canals on both sides had been designed by the same British engineers long before Partition. The manual labour, he added, came from the prisons of undivided Punjab.

The bus crossed a long bridge over the Raavi, which was bone-dry, most of its waters having been diverted by India through canals, based on the river water treaty signed thirteen years after Partition, the knowledgeable soil scientist informed them. At the time, Pakistan had expressed fears that during periods of war India could force it into submission simply by stopping its water supply, since all the rivers entered from India.

The bus passed through the narrow bazars of the temple town, the shops gaily decorated for the day and displaying finely crafted souvenirs. The wide majestic front of the gurudwara with its tall domes at each end came upon them rather suddenly. There was a sprawling front garden, complete with a fountain obliterating the view of the temple. Inside, the rectangular sarovar had a wide marble floor all around it, covered with men, fully dressed women and kids taking a holy dip. These were Sikhs from Canada who had arrived ahead of the Indian contingent. The rows of rooms with arched fronts around the periphery reminded Prakash of the Golden Temple at Amritsar.

They were ushered into a long corridor for a noisy lunch, where people sat in neat lines and were served by local volunteers. Turbaned boys and girls with covered heads moved briskly between the lines, insisting that the guests take another helping. Prakash heard comments about how the chillies tasted hotter and potatoes blander 'this side'. In that cacophony of colours, sounds, tastes and smells, with enthralled men and women talking about real and imagined differences in vegetables on the two 'sides', Prakash remembered his first visit to Pakistan, which had lasted just a few minutes.

~

He had been nine when his school had taken the students out of Amritsar for a picnic. The four hundred boys were taken in buses to an orchard twenty miles from the city, abutting the border with Pakistan. The orchard had belonged to a student's father and had been lent to the school for the day on the assurance that the picnickers would not pluck any oranges. This was easier said than done. The teachers spent most of the day chasing the kids. In the melee, Prakash and two older boys managed to slip away to take a look at the border.

They did not have far to go. Soon, they saw conical pillars placed so far apart from each other that it was hard to tell if they were supposed to form a row. One of the boys pointed to the orchard on the other side of the pillars and whispered, 'That is Pakistan!' Jaws dropped.

Prakash found this hard to believe. There was no police, no army, and no barbed wire in sight. The only other person was an old gardener in a black cap, plucking ripe oranges on the other side and throwing them onto a heap. He turned from his work and smiled at the boys with a gleam in the old eyes.

'Want some oranges?' he asked, across the thirty feet that separated them. Prakash nodded, his heart thumping.

'Then come and take,' he said with a wide smile, his wrinkles deepening.

The boys walked across quickly, looking in both directions, as if they were crossing a busy road. They pulled their shirt-tails out of their shorts and held them together in front as the gardener filled the makeshift baskets with oranges. In a stern voice, yet with the smile that deepened his wrinkles and showed a gap in his teeth, he told them, 'Now, off you go, back to your India. Fast!'

The boys scampered back, holding their treasures in front of them, a loud guffaw following them. The nine-year-old Prakash found it amusing that when somebody laughed in Pakistan, you could hear it in India.

The teacher who saw them first was livid, 'You were told ten times not to touch the oranges.' Prakash was on the verge of defending himself, when a look from the other boys made him shut up. They quietly accepted the reprimand and surrendered their gift, which was added to the heap

of confiscated Indian oranges which had to be given back
to the orchard owner, with apologies. When the teachers
were at lunch, Prakash tried to pick out a Pakistani orange
to take home as a memento for his parents, but soon gave
up. He was very surprised that Pakistani oranges could not
be told apart from the Indian ones.

~

Dormitories were allotted in the gurudwara and Prakash
found himself lying on a worn mattress spread on a jute
cot, with his bag under his head. Despite the noises from
below and the constant recitation of a paath by the man on
his left, Prakash dozed off.

In the evening, after a long recitation of gurbani from the
holy book and yet another community meal, accompanied
by the singing of shabads, the Sikh hymns, the moonswept
courtyard of that four-hundred-year-old shrine was taken
over by an esoteric annual ritual. A microphone was set
up and a man in his eighties, wearing a formal sherwani,
welcomed the Indians in Punjabi which had a heavy Seraiki
accent. He reminded them that it was the only time of the
year when people from the Hindustani side of Punjab came
to Pakistan. He said it was a pity the two governments
were so stingy with visas that even the animals and birds
found it difficult to cross the border. He went on to pepper
the satire with examples: a monkey wearing a collar with
an Amritsar address had to undergo security clearance to
verify that it was not a spy when found on the Pakistani
side of the border; and a pigeon with Urdu markings had

been 'arrested' by the Indian police on suspicion of being a Pakistani 'agent'. Both examples were true and had been a source of delight to cartoonists on both sides. Hearty clapping followed, and the old man had the audience's full attention. He said that Muslims who had migrated to this side used this occasion to update themselves about the Hindu and Sikh friends they knew before Partition in the various cities where they had then lived. The names of the cities would be called out one by one, and if there were any Indians from that city, they were to step apart and meet the Pakistanis uprooted from there.

A young man in a long shirt and a salwar took the microphone. He would name a city in Indian Punjab and then pause to allow visitors from there to arise and step aside. Pakistanis from that city would surround them for news. A bonfire was lit and cardamom tea served. 'Amritsar... Patiala... Jalandhar... Ludhiana... Ambala... Hoshiarpur... Hissar... Bhatinda...' It went on, and one half of the courtyard emptied into the other, as people sat in huddles around bonfires, sipping tea and fine-tuning their locations as if zooming in on a map: 'No, not the main city, but the village Sakhowal, across the canal which skirts the city.'

Most of the people who asked questions were middle-aged or older. Every year in this manner, they attempted to fill the gaps in their heads about friends and neighbours they had left behind. Ailing fathers or grandfathers, too old to come, sent sons or nephews with questions that were read out by a youngster on the old relative's behalf. Precise questions were asked and sometimes answers found.

'What about Ram Lubhaya's son?'

'Married, has no children. He took over the workshop. It is a big factory now. Does not treat the father too well. The daughter got married and went to England.'

The full moon had moved up in the sky and there was a nip in the air. Bonfires had been lit all around the courtyard by now. Old men and women, and some young ones too, from 'this side' and from 'that side' sat huddled, asking question after question. News of a death was precious too. It filled a void.

'The railway line has a huge bridge over it now. You do not have to wait at the crossing.'

'Chander Prakash went to Dubai after Susheela passed away. His son works there. Remember, the one, who was born on Id?'

There was rambunctious shouting from another corner, where two schoolmates from a village near Jalandhar had found each other after decades. Wistful elders and curious youngsters with intense expressions pulled the shawls and blankets closer around them as the night went by.

Prakash found himself sitting cross-legged on the ground alone, rubbing his hands against the chill, with no bonfire near him. Everyone sitting around him had shifted to the other side of the courtyard. No Muslims had been torn away from his city, Chandigarh, simply because it did not exist at the time of Partition.

'Salam alekum,' somebody addressed him. Prakash replied 'Walekum salam,' peering in the dark to make out the faces.

They were young men. Three. Much younger than him, they sat on the ground. Salman and Mehmood appeared to be twins, but were brothers, two years apart. They worked in their father's jewellery shop very close by. Shaukat, who was a student in Lahore was visiting his friends in Nankana Sahib. When Prakash introduced himself, he exclaimed, 'Wow, a real shrink. But what are you doing here? You are not even a Sikh.'

'No, but my wife is,' Prakash said vaguely. He explained that he wanted to see Pakistan and would not have been allowed to any other way. Shaukat pointed at the bonfires dotting the gurudwara's courtyard and said wryly, 'You're not going to see Pakistan this way either. Come with us and we will show you around. We have a car.'

Prakash remembered the ominous visa stamp in his passport, 'The only other city I am allowed to visit is Lahore.'

Salman said, 'So, let us go to Lahore. We can all stay at Shaukat's.' Neither the offer nor his readiness to accept seemed strange to Prakash at the time.

He located Mohinder Singh in the Jalandhar huddle and asked for permission. Mohinder did not look too happy but reluctantly agreed. He knew of many instances of such impromptu hospitality on both sides of the border. Pakistanis who came to Indian cities to watch cricket and could not find hotel rooms were often taken home by Indian spectators whom they had just met in the stadium, while cheering for the opposite team. He told Prakash to join the group at Lahore in two days. Prakash left his passport with him for it to be stamped at the local police station, and then again in Lahore, as if it was the most natural thing to do, and went to the dormitory to collect his bag.

A yellow Chevorlet Impala, looking incongruous in that lane with its triple tail lights, was parked outside the gurudwara. It was a very old model, probably late fifties, Prakash thought, and earlier layers of paint showed in blue and maroon patches. Mehmood went to a paan shop and made a phone call to tell his parents that they would not be home that night. Then they set off—three Pakistanis and one Indian—for Lahore.

'Kishore or Rafi?' asked Shaukat at the wheel.

'Rafi,' Prakash said offhand, and the scratchy stereo started belting out the peppy, '*Phir wohi dil laya hoon*'.

An hour and a half later, Prakash crossed the bridge over the Raavi for the second time that day. They passed in front of the dazzlingly lit Royal Mosque built by Aurangzeb, said to be able to accommodate one lakh people at worship. For the next two hours, they drove around the city, stopping once by the roadside to change a tyre. They had a kebab dinner in the Anarkali Bazaar, which at night morphed into a sprawling sit-out food court. The Impala was then driven to Shaukat's house in Gawal Mandi.

None of them were aware that Gawal Mandi was the market that had shocked Dr Iqbal Junaid Hussain by its stillness on his last night alive, three decades ago. They climbed up a narrow staircase under the pale light of a street lamp, the same that Dr Hussain used to climb every three months to deposit his insurance premium at the Empire of India Assurance Company. Salman insisted on carrying Prakash's bag. The room was above a confectionery shop, but the market was shut and the street quiet. Shaukat pulled a key from under the mattress and unlocked a cupboard. From behind books on political science, he produced a bottle of Bagpiper whiskey.

'Who should we drink to,' he asked with a conspiratorial glint in his eye, as he poured out pegs for each of them, 'Gavaskar or Bedi?'

'Imran Khan,' promptly responded Prakash, as grins lit up the faces of the brothers opposite. When the laughter and cricketing talk finally died dow, an hour later, Salman and Mehmood slept on the floor. Prakash and Shaukat took the double bed, twenty miles from the border, which Prakash had first crossed as a forty-day-old infant, clinging to his mother.

~

He dreamt of Amritsar. He was fourteen, and it was pitch-dark on a freezing December morning. He had just emerged from a house in one of the convoluted lanes. His fingers groped the cold metal of the lock on his cycle and found the keyhole in a practised movement. He came here every morning at four to teach two cousins, a couple of years younger than him. He had to finish his own homework before getting ready for school. Teeth chattering, he pulled on his cotton gloves and started cycling briskly to his house. He'd discovered that if he paddled faster he felt less cold. Woollen gloves would have been better for the chill in the damp lanes, but it would have been difficult to get a grip on the handle—and the dark streets were already bustling with traffic.

The halwai shops were open, a huge black cauldron full of milk being heated over a charcoal fire outside each one. An inky darkness still prevailed, but people could be made out as their breath condensed in pale white puffs in the bitter chill. Prakash lived near the Golden Temple. Men and women with covered heads and bare feet were converging for morning prayers. Strains of music from the gurudwara mingled with bustling sounds from shops, as the tinkling bicycle bells of Amritsar mingled with those of early morning Lahore and woke Prakash up.

Prakash's hosts took him on another tour of the city. They went inside the Badshah Mosque and then crossed over into the mammoth Moghul Fort, built in layers by generations of Moghul and Sikh emperors. They drove to the tombs of Jahangir and his wife Noor Jahan. The tomb of Anarkali was now inside the Punjab government office complex. The ordinariness of the surroundings grated against the dancing, shimmery imagery of the iconic movie *Mughal-e-Azam*, a smash hit in both countries.

Shaukat finished the roasted corn-cob that he had been chewing and threw the core over the wall. He stood in the middle of the room and said theatrically, with chin up, as if he was Dilip Kumar facing a camera, 'Anarkali was taken prisoner, and I stood watching helplessly.'

Mehmood walked to a point below the pale dome, pretending to twirl his clipped moustache and thundered, 'What else could you have done, Prince? You are not the Emperor. I am!' It seemed they had done it before. Salman who had been cleaning his ear, threw away the matchstick, left the low parapet that he had been sitting on, ducking a peon with a stack of old files. He joined the other two and scolded Shaukat, 'Poaching your father's favourite concubine does not behove a Prince of the Mughal empire. Tut-tut. History will never forgive you.' Another peon carrying a tray with a glass and a bottle of Coca-Cola looked disapprovingly at the trio, now laughing and slapping one another's backs.

'We do another one in which Anarkali is a boy,' Salman informed Prakash. 'Want to watch that?' Prakash laughed and said, 'No thanks, I can imagine it.'

During an early lunch of keema-parantha from a cart near the tonga stand, Salman idly asked, 'Where were you born?' and Prakash remembered the things that his parents had told him, bit by bit , over the years as he grew up, some of which he told them.

* * *

Thirty-two-year-old Ved Kohli was a mild man, fully content with his world, which he divided equally between his school and his two-room house in Guru Nanak Pura. He was a history teacher at the Government High School, Gujranwala, a mid-sized city in undivided Punjab. Every morning, he left home at seven-thirty sharp, returning to

Sneh, his wife of three years, at two in the afternoon. A methodical man, he stuck to his clockwork routine, and expected the world to behave in a similar fashion. The only other city he had ever seen was Lahore, when he had chaperoned a group of students to the museum.

For a teacher of history, Ved was strangely oblivious to the winds of change swirling around him that summer of 1947. He did not like change. The only variation he had allowed himself in the last eight years was his marriage to Sneh, and the new bicycle that she had brought in her dowry.

That year, when school opened after summer break, he continued reaching for work at exactly eight in the morning, even though half the teachers and two-thirds of the students did not show up. He carried on teaching near-empty classrooms about the conquests of Alexander the Great and the causes of the downfall of the Mughal Empire. His eyes refused to take in the stabbings and killings that had already begun. If he saw a commotion on the street, he took another way home. There was talk of Partition being just weeks away, but he stubbornly believed that it was merely a rumour. Even if it was not, where was he supposed to go with his seven-month-pregnant wife? In any case, he thought recklessly, Gujranwala was bound to go to India.

By the beginning of July, even Ved could sense disquiet in the people around him, including his Muslim colleagues. When Mr Farooqi, the headmaster, asked meaningfully and out of concern, 'What is your "programme?"', all that

Ved could manage was, 'Home, after the last period.' The question, however, stayed with him.

The schools closed down for the second time that summer. When rioting and lynching began, the demand for trucks was very high as families wanted to travel with whatever belongings they could carry, across their best guess at the future dividing line between the two countries. More than half of the trucks were looted on their way to the border. Stories were rife about caravans where the young women had vanished, and everybody else had been stabbed to death. As the summer wore on, violent attacks became a fact of life, both inside and outside the city. After another two months, even if Ved Kohli had wanted to, he could not have left Gujranwala.

One early August night, Roshaan Bibi, the midwife, delivered their son. After the birth, Roshaan had to stay in Ved's house for two days, since the streets were treacherous even for Muslims. On the third day, when her husband Bashir came looking for her, she persuaded him to borrow a friend's jeep to take Ved, Sneh and the baby to their village, Rahwali, just outside Gujranwala.

According to mid-wifely wisdom, a newborn child is particularly vulnerable for the first forty days. The childless Muslim couple gave shelter to the Hindu family for those forty days, during which Sneh mostly lay motionless under a chadar, getting up only to nurse the baby. She couldn't stop thinking of the risk that the large-hearted couple were taking simply by keeping them in their house. For her, the enormity and uncertainty of their situation became combined with her postpartum blues, and she hardly even spoke during those days, though Roshaan insisted that she eat and drink properly, alternately scolding and cajoling nourishing food into her on a daily basis. Prakash knew that Sneh remembered that brief hiatus in her life very well; whenever he fell ill, his mother would cook the warm besan and ghee sheera that Roshaan had made for her so often during that anxious period.

One sweltering afternoon, during a lull in the bloodbath, the friend's jeep was requisitioned again. Ved and his family were taken by Bashir and Roshaan to the T-junction on the highway. Ved kept an eye out for a Pakistani army vehicle going towards the border. Sitting in the back seat of the jeep, Sneh had dozed off with Prakash—Roshaan had given him the name—feeding under her dupatta. An army truck stopped. To help Sneh get down, Ved tried to take Prakash from her grasp. Sneh, exhausted and on edge, felt a tug at her breast as the tiny lips refused to let go. She woke up with a start, panicking that the child was being pulled away. Roshaan soothed her, stroking her forehead and shoulders, and helping her down off the jeep. She boarded the truck with the help of a Pakistani soldier, retrieved her child from Roshaan and, as the baby resumed its interrupted meal, they travelled towards India.

* * *

'Gujranwala is only an hour away. How can we not go?' Mehmood said excitedly.

'No visa,' Prakash reminded him.

'It is only a few hours. We will be in and out,' Shaukat said. He added, 'Your mother will be so happy.'

~

Within two hours, they were in Gujranwala. Prakash rang up his mother from a post office, the postmaster hovering while he talked. He told her that he was in Gujranwala and had already seen the college where his father had studied. Sneh's voice trembled when he asked her about the address of the house where they had lived, but she rattled it off, '108, Urdu Bazar, Guru Nanak Pura.'

The young men found it easily. The name of the colony was still the same, so was the name of the street. Even the house number had not changed. Eerily, the man living there was a history teacher too, and in the same school. He was as old as Prakash. Tea and biscuits were served and photographs taken. The house had been rebuilt, but a wall in the back still had the original small porous bricks. When Prakash passed his hand over the wall. It felt cold and damp, even in the heat.

They asked for directions to Rahwali, which was now a part of the city. Although the Impala got stuck in the muddy lanes, the news that somebody had come from India looking for Roshaan Dai preceded them. Neighbours and street urchins were eager to see the visitors and give directions to her house.

When they reached it, seventy-year-old Roshaan stood straight and tall in the door frame. She looked at the four boys and came straight to Prakash, embracing him as naturally as if they had met many times in the intervening years. When he awkwardly tried to explain that he could not bring any gifts because he never thought he'd be able to visit her, Roshaan waved her hand dismissively, 'Your coming is a gift. In this village, for the next two months we are going to talk only about you.'

* * *

The Impala was now stuck in Lahore's infamous evening traffic at Gawal Mandi. Prakash's mind went back to Roshaan, who had shown him around the three-room house 'where you spent the first forty days of your life.'

After the first flurry of welcome, they had settled into a comfortable conversation, asking for and exchanging stories, while the other three went foraging in the Impala for mithai to mark the occasion. Eventually, Prakash had told her about Ved's death.

The summer of 1975 had been particularly blistering in the plains of North India. Prakash and Jasmeet had been married for six months and were in Amritsar on one of their regular visits. Over a late breakfast of paranthas, the family heard on the radio that Prime Minister Indira Gandhi had declared a state of Emergency in the country. A ten-minute discussion about the pros and cons of the Emergency ensued, during which Ved had given his opinion that some good might come of it, in the form of better discipline in government offices, while the others remained noncommittal. Once Sneh asked about dinner, the Kohli household was done with the topic of the

Emergency. Ved had volunteered to cook mutton, which was his signature dish. The process started with him going out and buying all the ingredients himself, as he held that buying the right cuts of mutton for each dish was an art.

After tea, while it was still hot and sunny outdoors, Ved had stepped out with his jute shopping bag. An hour later, a commotion outside the house alerted Sneh that something was wrong. She ran out barefoot. There had been a protest rally against the Emergency in Hall Bazaar. Someone was carrying a pistol and had fired a shot in the air as a show of defiance. The police became jittery and fired back above the heads of the crowd. This broke up the procession, but one stray bullet hit a passer-by, who died immediately, still clutching his jute bag. Prakash and some of his neighbours rushed to the bazaar. By the time they got there, the police had removed the body. What Prakash saw was the chalk outline of his father's body on the road, surrounded by stray onions, tomatoes, and a jute bag with the freshly cut pieces of mutton.

Ved was the most apolitical person in the whole world. He accepted life as it came, whether that meant looking for the positive side to the Emergency or ignoring the pangs of Partition. He had settled in Amritsar, because it was the first city that lay beyond the border, and he did not feel a need to explore further. He had small ambitions and simple desires. The only desire that he'd had that day was to impress his daughter-in-law with his mutton rogan josh. *Surely, nobody should be shot for that*, Prakash thought, as anger took over him.

He told Roshaan that, a few days later, he'd driven his motorcycle in the pre-dawn darkness to the Raavi, and dropped his father's ashes in the river which flowed to Pakistan. He didn't mention that when he returned, he'd clung to Jasmeet and cried inconsolably.

He wasn't sure how much Roshaan had understood, but after he'd finished speaking, she'd thrown up her hands and said, 'He might as well have stayed. He might even have been alive. Who knows?'

'It is stupid but one wonders!' Roshaan continued. She began to reminisce. 'He was shy, but when they stayed in this house, those days, he often talked to me. And he told me that he did not want to leave...he even asked if there was any way the three of you could stay back. I talked to Bashir (God bless his soul!), who talked to his friends, some of whom knew people who mattered. They guaranteed safety, but there was talk of changing religion... Ved was willing. I remember what he said: "Religion is not important to me. It would be like changing socks." But Sneh became even more withdrawn...she was not talking much those days anyway. That sometimes happens after childbirth. I think Ved sensed her pain and gave up the idea.'

As if reminded of something, she got up suddenly and left the room, saying, 'Just a minute'. There was a picture on the wall facing Prakash's chair. He got up to have a closer look. It was a charcoal sketch of a man in his forties, the thick dark hair parted in the middle, a naughty glint in the eyes, a bushy moustache with hint of a twirl at each end and a short beard. There was a tiny self-effacing signature in a corner of the sketch, partly hidden by the frame. Prakash could make out 'Roshaan'.

He hurried back to his chair, just before Roshaan returned, carrying a flat papier-mâché box. Its purple colour had long faded and the surface was chipped. Roshaan pulled at the rusted clip. Inside, was a necklace, a delicate gold and kundan piece, finely crafted and studded with blue-, green- and honey-coloured stones, lying snugly in a mould of maroon velvet.

Prakash looked up questioningly.

'It is your mother's. The day you left, what with all the hurry, and Bashir blowing his horn every few seconds, since the jeep had to be returned, this was left lying under Sneh's pillow. I did not have any way to contact her, or any address to send it to... I know that this came from Ved's mother, who had got it from her mother-in-law. She will be happy to have it back.' Roshaan put it in his lap and Prakash held it awkwardly, dumbfounded.

Roshaan smiled down at him and then asked abruptly, 'Do you have a rather prominent belly button?'

He blushed and said haltingly, 'Yes... but how do you know?'

'Because I am the cause of it. The night I delivered you in the Guru Nanak Pura house, the electricity went off and we had to manage with an oil lamp. That alone would not have been a problem. You took a while, but I did deliver you nice and safe. But there was a mob carrying mashaals and yelling like all the fiends in Hell as they rampaged through the lane, barely five feet from where you were being born. I was trembling all over when I tied the cord. Normally my handiwork is much better.'

~

Prakash looked mesmerized at the jalebis being swirled into boiling oil in the doorway of a halwai's shop, as the Impala idled in the traffic. He took out the papier-mâché box from the flap at the back of the seat for another look at the unexpected family heirloom. As he self-consciously touched his navel through his shirt, he felt sure that Sneh had deliberately forgotten to pack her necklace. He knew she would not be too happy about getting it back, but he could not have risked dimming the glow which had appeared on Roshaan's face at the sight of him. Besides he was just the messenger boy. If Sneh wanted to thank Roshaan, she would have to bring her a gift herself, properly, in person.

PARTITIONING MADNESS

'This is weird, even by the standards of madness. I go to sleep in a mental hospital and wake up on a cold railway platform. "Wake up" is a relative term. My mind is muddled and thinking tiresomely sticky. A throbbing headache stops my thoughts from connecting with each other.

'It is a frosty winter morning and I am at this railway station in a collarless black shirt, a grey pyjama and a coarse pullover which reaches my knees. I look around. I am surrounded by hundreds of similarly clad silhouettes moving in and out of a dense fog, which has somehow seeped into my head too. A train quietly glides into the station and a subdued murmur travels like a ripple from one end of the platform to the other. A sharp hiss from the steam engine startles the dervish-like figures which float back into the fog, taking me along, away from the platform edge.

'Heat from the steam engine does the trick. The fog quickly melts away, even from my head. Even the pulsating pain in the temples which had been chopping at my new-born thoughts comes haltingly to a stop, and I know exactly what has been happening. Right away, three things are as clear to me as the huge black-on-yellow Lahore Junction sign in English, Hindi, Punjabi and Urdu.

'One, that I, Rulda Singh, am one of the four hundred and fifty 'non-Muslim lunatics' being shifted from Pakistan to India more than three years after the actual Partition of 1947. The non-Muslim lunatics forgotten in Pakistan, and still alive three years later have been collected from Hyderabad, Peshawar and Lahore—the three mental hospitals of Pakistan. All this, Fattu and I had picked up in the last few weeks, from overhearing conversations while sitting on the long bench outside the medical superintendent's office.

'Second, I know that it is a Wednesday, because that was when this interchange was supposed to have happened.

'And the third is that the headache and frozen haze in the brain that have just melted away indicate that I have been given electric convulsive treatment this morning. Mondays, Wednesdays and Fridays are "bijli" days at Lahore Mental Hospital and, knowing them as I do, I didn't expect the authorities to let the minor issue of relocation to another country interrupt an on-going course of treatment—particularly when that country is all of thirty minutes away. I touch my temple with a finger and look at the sticky paste they apply so that the current passes smoothly into the brain. They are supposed to wipe it clean afterwards, but of course, they never do.

'Now I also know why Fattu had not come to the gate to say goodbye. If he had, he would have cried so much that I would have remembered, ECT or no ECT. It was not because all the Muslim patients were to be locked away in their wards that morning to prevent any of them from wrongly joining the queues in the courtyard. Fattu would have found a way, using all his guile and cigarettes as bribe. He must have been recovering from his own bolt of hundred volts, lying unconscious in some dark recess of the ECT room, with the nurses and orderlies busy with the hospital's biggest send-off in the fifty years of its existence.'

~

'Fattu's course of ECT had started when he stopped eating, praying, sleeping and replying to questions, even from me. Then one evening, he was found lying at the bottom of a well at the far end of the wheat fields. He was discovered half-drowned in ice-cold water by a scraggy stray pup, which had stood, yelping, on the parapet, till a bunch of patients came running.

'When I'd asked him the reason for jumping into the well, he had said, "I wanted to make a token contribution towards balancing the statistics." He has this wry smile, particularly while being cryptic, which was often lately. "Zubaid Mian, the head clerk, says that the death rate of non-Muslim lunatics in the last three years has been twice than was expected."

'"What is expected, Fattu? People die unexpectedly all the time." I get exasperated, because he continues to smile.

'"Train will go empty if it is delayed even more," he says while being pulled away by two attendants and locked up for the night.

'My own course of ECTs had been ordered because the hospital ran out of anti-lice powder. When I went to the harried head warden, Suleiman, with my beard and hair flowing, asking for some lice powder, he'd snapped, "There isn't enough powder to go around. Why don't you get your hair trimmed and have a shave or something? You Sikhs have hair of gold or what!" I remembered my mother telling me about a Sikh's hair being sacred when I was fourteen. This was after she had slapped me hard when I had snipped a tuft off my side-burn just for the heck of it.

'I'd glared down at Suleiman and caught him by the grubby collar which always smells of paraldehyde. I'd let go abruptly as I realized the horror of what I'd done. Suleiman fell down and I sheepishly helped him get up. That ended my status as one of the two discharged-but-uncollected patients, the other, of course, being Fattu. This was three years and four months after Dr Iqbal Junaid Hussain (God bless his soul), had discharged us and, when nobody came to "collect" us, had told us to stay on and "be useful".

'In less than half an hour, my case file has been located and three and a half years of dust on it cleaned. It looks too neat to me, as I stand before the Deputy Medical Superintendent, who always has a stethoscope slung around his neck. I had once asked Fattu, "What does he hear with that?" and Fattu had replied with a straight face, "Voices."

'While seeing the worryingly new-looking file, the nervousness and mirth over Fattu's joke coalesce to project a foolish smile on my face. No other doctor likes the Day

Deputy because he is an Urdu-speaking Mohajir from Meerut and not a Punjabi. Every other day he'd find a slip of paper on his table advising him to go to Karachi, where all the non-Punjabi refugees from India went to settle, or so they said. The Deputy shouts at me, "What tickles you? Please share the joke." I sense that I am in deep trouble. I know from experience that answers bring even more abrasive questions.

"'Do you think Suleiman is a patient and you the head warden? Has the world turned upside down all of a sudden? And why did you hit and cut his lip with your steel kara? The government of Pakistan tolerantly permits it as a tribal totem," the Deputy says venomously, "You cannot use it as a weapon!"

'I try to tell him I have not worn a kara for a long time, putting my hands up to show him my empty wrists, but out of fear my mouth is like sandpaper and no words come out.

"'So, you destroyed the evidence. Very clever, no?" Without waiting for an answer, he signs the admission form converting my Discharged status to Admitted with a quick flourish. He then becomes all reason and cool logic. "We would have had to admit you anyway in a couple of weeks. We can send only patients admitted with us to India, not any loose cannons loitering around. Can we?" Even I find that reasonable, till I hear what follows.

"'But we cannot readmit you without a valid reason, can we now? That would be illegal, no? So, I am writing 'Acute Mania' as the diagnosis, knowing fully well that you have nothing of the sort." With his lips pursed, he added, "With Violent Tendencies". I can read from where I stand. "Just to justify readmission; doesn't mean anything actually. I have just printed your ticket to India. Say thank you."

'And then, tapping the glass table with the chest piece of his stethoscope, he says, "And if you are that ill, we are bound by duty, to treat you effectively. Aren't we? It will be unethical if we don't." Mumbling to himself, he jots down "ECT" in the treatment column. The three letters look as big and as shaky to me as the title at the start of the war movie they showed us in the compound the other night. I am nudged by the orderly towards my old ward, number 12, like a recidivist felon being taken back to prison. As I turn to say goodbye, I see the doctor put my file in the outbound tray for the magistrate's signature. He picks up a slip of paper lying near his feet, reads it, rolls it into a pill and throws it viciously out of the door over my head. I pick it up. It reads, "Go to Karachi, you sweaty, stinky Mohajir."

'A benevolent electric shock is the parting gift that I carry in my head from my erstwhile carers. I would be told later in Amritsar that somebody had put an asterisk on the cover of my case file with a note: "Next ECT due on Friday, 8 December, 1950". It was presumed that a carefully thought-out treatment plan would be executed seamlessly, notwithstanding the cross-border dislocation. Also implied was a supercilious assumption that doctors on both sides understood each other even if the politicians did not.

'If somebody had taken care to sift through our thick dog-eared files it would be quickly known to him that the two peaks of illnesses—Fattu's and mine—had not only respectfully steered clear of each other all these years, but were also exactly the reverse of each other in every manner. It was for the first time that we had "fallen ill" together. In fact, for over three years, both of us had been, in Fattu's words, as "squeaky healthy" as any gentleman member of the Officers' Club in Hoshiarpur, where Fattu had worked as a boy. Earlier, my "boisterous excitements" kicked in twice a year, coinciding with the change of seasons, whereas Fattu's dark depressions occurred at the peak of summer and winter. With awe, each of us had watched the other's illness from close quarters, the reverse of our own. It was like looking at the mirror image of a mountain in still waters. Of course, we had our add-ons: mine were visions, and Fattu's, voices.'

* * *

'After a particularly long screech, the empty train had come to a stop and I had found myself standing next to the third compartment from the rear. With an eye on the large black trunk which contained patients' files, the guard hung a red flag from the side of the cabin. A subdued thrill of sorts appeared on the faces of the drab crowd, which, I only then noticed, did have a smattering of turbans from the Peshawar contingent.

'The mass of people had surged towards the seven compartments marked "General" and the three marked

"Ladies". The train was dripping wet after a wash and smelled clean. The words "Pakistan Railways" had been painted over the still-visible "North Western Railway".

'The train from Hyderabad had already reached Lahore the previous day. "Charya Express has arrived," the new house doctor had announced to the medical superintendent, as if announcing important guests at a wedding. "Charya", of course, is "mad" in Sindhi. The house doctor, now anxious about arrangements, had carried on, "There are fifty-five men and twenty-three women, sir. Where will they sleep?"

'They had finally slept on the floor in the waiting hall of the outpatients' department. "Don't worry about arrangements for the patients on the bus from Peshawar. It will go straight to the gurudwara. They are all Sikhs," the superintendent had said, to calm his younger colleague's anxieties.'

~

'Although Fattu and I had been stripped of our honorary status and we were now supposed to sleep in the ward as patients, help in the kitchen and take part in 'agricultural therapy' , there was a deal of sorts. We were allowed to continue sleeping on benches in the office veranda, which was now walled-in, an extra room with many windows. On our part, we had to tidy up the offices before the doctors came and run errands for them during the day, because Taufeeq, the peon, had gone for a pilgrimage to Ajmer Sharif across the border and had not come back. The rumour was that Taufeeq, having sampled life in both the countries, had made a considered choice and stayed in India even after his visa expired. Another rumour, which his second wife, Miriam, believed in, was that it was not the call of the Pir Murshid which had pulled him back but that of his doe-eyed and childless first wife, whose picture he had kept safely between the folds of his brand-new Pakistani driving license. She had dug in her heels and refused to come with them to Pakistan. Miriam was raring to cross the border and drag her husband back, but the Indian High Commission had refused to give her visa, citing her husband's visa violation as the reason.

'When the fifty-five patients from Peshawar arrived at the gurudwara, along with their Pathan doctor, one of the Sikhs ran around the marble quadrangle, perplexed. He began shouting profane curses at the boys flying kites from the house tops around the gurudwara. It was obvious that he had been here before. From his standpoint, four spires should have been standing majestically at the corners of a wide open expanse of ground. Looking at the gurudwara hemmed in on three sides by freshly built houses and a new mosque, the pot-bellied Sikh with psychosis reacted as if personally violated. Crying like a child, with fists rubbing his eyes, he unleashed a tirade of curses, interspersed with sobs and loud clearings of the nose, his colourful turban now askew. Soon, the abuses got too explicit, involving the near relatives of the people living next to the gurudwara. Fearing a riot, the old man was overpowered by the younger patients, taken inside the sanctum-sanctorum and given an injection on his plentiful behind by the Pathan doctor.

'All this I had heard while we were lying on the benches after dinner, from Fattu who, in turn, had overhead the conversation between the Day Deputy and the Pathan doctor. "These Sikhs!" was all that the Deputy had said, it seems.

'After passing on the account of the Sikh, Fattu, who had recovered remarkably well after five ECTs, gave me an unrelated jab, "Sleep well, Ruldia. This is your last night in the land of the pure. Tomorrow you sleep in the country of the impure, deservedly so, you kaffir." The impish smile which accompanied such needling was missing that day.

'Neither of us spoke after that, but each knew that the other was awake. My throat was parched. Water was prohibited the night before a morning ECT, to avoid choking on vomit while knocked out. Fattu spoke from inside the blanket he had pulled up to cover his face, although the windows were shut and it was not cold at all, "Didn't I tell you that people 'outside' are very smart? They are sending you to where my home is and keeping me where your home is. Could we have matched that?" I kept quiet. We had gone over that before.

'Fattu took the blanket off his face, pointed at the pale half-moon beyond the window panes and said, "The other half of the moon has gone to your country. You will see it tomorrow, Ruldu. The Urdu paper had said at the time of Partition that it was the biggest exchange of people in the history of mankind. You should be proud that you are a part of it. 'General Rulda Singh, who led his battalion of four hundred and fifty mental patients across the Wagah Pass into India' is how history will remember you."

"'The big exchange happened three years ago", I reminded him.

"'It started then but it is not finished. Mentals are the rear end of mankind."

"'Are we mankind? Do we count even as the rear end?" I asked.

"'Of course we count. Even the tables and chairs count. The horses count. Everything that can be counted counts and has to be meticulously counted and fairly divided between the two countries. Even us." It had become an entirely different line of conversation.

'With a jerk of the blanket indicating a good night of sorts, Fattu buried his face. I asked the bulge under the blanket, "Then why were we not asked about our preference? Everybody else was. Government employees were asked which country they wanted to be allotted to. Even the prisoners in jails were asked to choose the country where they wanted to be imprisoned."

'Fattu's voice sounded sleepy. The urge to cry seemed to have passed and his head came out again, "Raumish says we were not asked because we have no legal capacity. We don't understand implications."

'This was a new topic between us and I was curious. "You mean even the Muslim patients have no legal capacity."

"'Even them. Legal capacity is secular. Like Quaid-e-Azam," Fattu muttered, pretending to be half-asleep.

'I asked, "You mean people outside understand the implications of everything they decide to do?"

"'Rulda, you are matriculate, but don't know a thing. Of course they do. That is how they are different."

"'So they knew a million people might die and still went ahead."

'Fattu replied, "Yes, they thought it was still worth it. They knew the implications, weighed the pros and cons and decided in a cool, detached manner and went ahead."

'I said interestedly, "The ones who stabbed and shot men, women and children must also have weighed the pros and cons, and coolly turned around 'implications' in their minds, before they killed or raped."

'There was a long pause.

'I thought of talking to Raumish, the nurse who took law classes, about it. But then I remembered that I would be gone before she came for work. Fattu was now sobbing without any pretence, making the blanket move like jelly. I got up, filled up the brass glass with water and kept drinking till the bottom of the glass was pointing at the pale half-moon. I hoped that I would choke on the ECT table. For the first time in many years, I remembered the night when I was five and the river had entered the village... I, too, started sobbing, telling myself that it was not for Fattu but for my long-gone father.'

~

'The surge of black and grey uniforms with its sprinkling of pink and purple swayed towards the train and was nudged into queues by men of the Punjab Border Police who were armed to the teeth as if going into a battle.

'After a perfunctory whistle, the train started moving, but just before it could clear the outer signal, there were several jerks and it ground to a stop with a protesting screech. A long whistle shrilled, split into two, signalling distress. Looking through the bars, I could just make out the figure of a rotund sardar wearing an outsized turban. He was running with surprisingly long steps, through the row of shanties bordering a ground full of soot and coal heaps. The uniformed young man who had jumped after him could not catch up because of the heavy rifle. It seemed that the need to do something about his shrunk temple had usurped any desire that the devout Sikh had ever had of going to a new country, where nobody, either man or god, knew him.

'The train guard was walking restlessly along the train, peering after the runaway. When it was clear that the sardar was going to outpace his pursuer, he shrugged his shoulders and furiously waved the green flag. Yet another long whistle, and the train jerked into motion once again. At the railway crossing, a school boy wearing a monkey cap that came down to his chin waved at everybody with gusto.'

* * *

Rulda stopped speaking. The three of them the Medical Superintendent Dr. Mohinder Singh, Prakash and Rula had been sitting in a tin-roofed veranda outside the Medical Superintendent's office when a freak hailstorm came up. Prakash had been posted to the Mental Hospital as an intern. They picked up their stools and ran inside, as fist-sized hail hit the tin like cannon balls, even while the afternoon sun shone brightly in another part of the sky.

For an hour, Rulda had been sitting straight, his hands clasped tightly in his lap, as if to stop himself from making gestures while he talked. His eyes, sharp and intense in the beginning, had become blurred and distant as he narrated, slowly, haltingly. Gradually his hands had let go of each other. He had passed his fingers through his greying beard as he talked, sitting on a makeshift stool he'd crafted himself in the hospital workshop.

As the three of them settled inside Dr Singh's office, Rulda served them piping hot samosas from the kitchen and resumed his story. Surrounded by rain, hail and sun on that freakish July afternoon, he opened his mouth just enough when he spoke, as if he felt self-conscious about his swollen gums, or so Prakash thought.

* * *

'Right away, green fields with a hint of brown began speeding past on both sides of the train, as far as one could see. Across the aisle sat Venky, a dark, frail boy who had not eaten anything on his own for years and spoke only a few Tamil words which nobody understood. Nobody knew either, how he had landed in Lahore, except that he was found at the railway station gesticulating and shouting furiously at a gaggle of burqa-clad women, in a language which a passer-by vaguely recognized as "Madrasi". A slip of paper found in his pocket had had a name but no address.

'One end of the thin rubber tube which went through his nose to the stomach was attached to his forehead with a sticking tape. On the tape, a nurse had scribbled in black ink "Milk, 10 oz, 7 a.m." hoping that her counterpart on the other side, would give him his next feed four hours later. Venky was looking spellbound at something outside the train and when I followed his gaze, I was startled by the sight of turbaned heads and bearded faces bobbing up and down outside the windows on both sides. They were Indian cavalry men escorting the train after it crossed the border, as if ushering in an exalted dignitary. It was routine work for the East Punjab Armed Police to ride alongside the trains entering India, to prevent opium runners from throwing gunny bags from the train into the bushes. The horsemen disappeared from the windows as a railway platform appeared.

'Venky abruptly stood up on his seat and shouted "Madras", his eyes wide and face lit up. The tube on his forehead had come undone because of the activity and I had to put it back in place, "Attari, not Madras, Venky. But yes, India."

'Venky did not find "India" interesting and sat back in his seat looking even more forlorn than before. Another train carrying Muslim mental patients gathered from hospitals across India had already arrived on the parallel track and curious men and women were trying to peep into windows of the incoming train. I had the urge to touch the other train and pass my fingers over the letters of "East Punjab Railways" painted over the still faintly visible "North Western Railways." Just then, the door of our compartment was unbolted and swung open.

'It was a small railway station with just two platforms connected by a high footbridge, which on that day served as the site of exchange for the mental patients. The process was quite like the exchange of prisoners of war, complete with queues, uniforms and names being ticked off from smudged lists on chipped clipboards. The lists were hastily written and several names on the carbon copies had to be guessed. The instructions were not to be fussy.

'The flat portion of the footbridge held several office tables joined end to end, and covered with white bedsheets, each stamped with NWR for North Western Railways. The sheets had been borrowed from the station master's house. The tables separated the two rows of Muslim and non-Muslim patients crossing over to the other platform, to the other train and into another country. Great care had been taken to keep the two streams separate, since patients from both sides looked similar, wore similar uniforms and almost everybody's hands trembled because of cold, apprehension and medicines. At least a thousand people were milling around by the bridge, which had been divided along its length with a thick rope. The long table in the middle was itself divided by a row of flower vases with fresh marigolds.

'We were made to put thumb-prints (and an occasional signature) on one of the two registers lying on the table. The doctor from Peshawar, in a suit and tie, sat next to a balding colleague from Amritsar. Indian Punjab had been left with no mental hospital after Partition and a detention centre, used to house offenders belonging to the Criminal Tribes, had been expanded in record time to receive the guests from Pakistan.

'I was outside the compartment holding up Venky, who was standing barefoot on the cold platform and shivering. Venky, as a matter of principle, refused to wear any footwear. A stretcher with Red Cross markings was being carried out of the next compartment and I realized that only patients on stretchers filled that compartment. As the stretcher passed by, I saw that the patient was a woman, in the middle of a massive seizure. Her face was a dirty blue and a trail of blood seeped from the corner of her mouth. The policemen, unused to this line of duty, ran with the stretcher to find the doctor, who was at the other door of the same compartment, trying to help a man whose fractured leg was plastered at such an angle that it wouldn't go through the door frame. The patient himself was of no help, as he kept shouting that he wanted to go back to Data Darbar in Lahore, where the police had found him running around the dargah undressed, singing ribald songs and stealing sweets. But the fracture had come later—I'd seen it happen after an argument with the kitchen staff.

'"You again! You have had four chapatis!"

'"Just one more please. I sing songs. I feel hungry, please." He had touched the cook's elbow pleadingly. The cook had shoved him back with force, making him trip over a bench and fall.

'When my queue reached the table in the middle of the footbridge, I signed the register. Across the table, in the row of men from India, a fragile figure with no moustache and a small pointed beard gave me a broad smile. The bright red tilak pasted on his forehead looked out of place. He explained without being asked, seeing my eyes lingering on the tilak, "Have always gone to Hanuman temple on Tuesdays since I was a kid, used to go from Bareilly hospital too. Last night in Amritsar, ran away from the hospital. It was nearby."

'"Chacha, wipe it off. They won't like it there," I advised him. As I pointed westward over his shoulder to Lahore, I passed a small slip under my palm to the Lahore-bound Hanuman bhakt, muttering, "Give it to Fattu."'

* * *

Of the non-Muslim patients received from Pakistan, the 282 Punjabis would be housed in Mental Hospital, Amritsar. The rest of the non-Punjabi patients were put on another train, for a much longer journey of two whole days and nights, to a mental hospital in Ranchi tucked away in the eastern corner of the country.

How the authorities managed to sift out the Punjabis from the non-Punjabis, when many of the patients had not spoken for years and would stare back blankly when asked any question, is not known. Their admission records would not have been of any help, since a large number of addresses were now on the 'other' side. What is known is that Venky, probably because he liked what was fed to him through his nasal tube in Amritsar, did not stand up and shout 'Madras' for those two days. He was left in Amritsar thanks to a faded carbon copy. A rushed peon, having wrestled with hundreds of Punjabi names already, peered briefly at the flimsy sheet and, in the dim light of the sorting office, wrote out Vikram Singh Chawla instead of Venkat S. Cholagar.

* * *

After a long pause, Prakash asked the Medical Superintendent whether it was true that half the patients that were supposed to be sent to India had died during the three years between Partition and the actual exchange. Rulda had gone back into the kitchen, and the two of them were left to contemplate the vivid colours of the sky at sunset. Dr Singh watched the red clouds glow and fade like embers before he replied.

'Well, it is true that we were expecting more patients.'

'How many came?'

'Four hundred and fifty.'

'How many did you expect?'

'More than twice as many.'

'Based on what?'

'There were written reports. Patients were there.'

'Can I see these sometime?'

'If I can find the papers. It has been twenty-two years.'

'What happened to the rest?'

'They died.'

'How can four hundred and fifty patients die in three years?'

'The Lahore hospital report of 1947 says it was cholera.'

'Would cholera kill just one religion?'

'GOK'

'GOK?'

'God only knows. I know that I do not want to know. It is time to move on.'

SITA'S BUS

Sialkot could be heavenly in November, thought Firdaus Cheema, despite feeling somewhat cramped in a salwar-kameez, with a t-shirt and loose slacks hidden under it, and a burqa worn over it, as she walked back from school. Firdaus was a physical training instructor at the Convent of Jesus and Mary, one of the oldest convent schools, even in undivided India. She was quite an achiever herself: one of the very few women physical training instructors, having done a 'proper' diploma from her hometown, Jullundur, which was now in India. At twenty-three she had been married twice. Also, this was her second religion, even though by an eerie quirk of chance her last name had not changed after either her first or second marriage.

Her mother-in-law insisted that Firdaus wear a burqa. Firdaus thought it was hardly any protection, expertly dodging a man with a flowing beard who swerved abruptly towards her in the narrow lane at the last moment. 'No chance, Maulana!' Firdaus chuckled to herself. Fleet shoes were useful. In the morning, she was picked up from Imam Sahib Chowk by the school van, but in the afternoon she preferred to walk rather than linger on at the school for another hour, waiting for its return trip.

~

Harpreet Cheema, the only child of Subedar Rajinder Singh Cheema, a single parent, had been married off at the age of twenty-one to Manjeet Cheema who owned a transport business in Sialkot. The marriage party had come from Sialkot to Jullundur in two buses owned by the bridegroom, and returned the same day. Harpreet was tall, fair and athletic. While growing up at a string of the army stations where her father was posted over the years, she had begun to take part in strenuous sports, often joining the boys for practice, and sometimes beating them too. Volleyball was her forte. Manjeet, on the other hand, was a bit on the plump side and an inch or two shorter than her, although the turban more than made up for that.

In the bus, Harpreet had excitedly watched the landscape go by. Any travel did that to her, even though she had not just travelled to but lived in far-flung places all over the country. She had not yet spoken a word, since she had not been spoken to. That had taken some effort. Her anxious father, aware of her chirpy nature, had instructed her to hold her tongue. 'Otherwise, they will think that I did not bring you up properly. Newly-wed girls are supposed to be demure,' he had fussed nervously.

The road was flanked mile after mile by rust-brown fields, and soon she had become bored by the monotony of

it. The ride had been bumpy and she'd been tossed about
in her seat. Accidentally at first, and then playfully, she'd
nudged Manjeet on the calf with the point of her sandal.
He'd looked at her scandalized, squirmed uneasily and
pulled his feet under the seat. When the bus stopped on
the other side of the Raavi bridge, Manjeet had gone out
for a while. His mother, who had been sitting on the other
side of him, had slid up to Harpreet.

'Since you insisted about the job, we sent your
application to the Sisters at the Convent. They said that
they will be happy to interview you.'

Harpreet had acknowledged the information with a
demure nod, noticing for the first time that her mother-
in-law was wearing far more gold than she was. Patting
the flower-shaped gold tikka so that it stayed at the centre
of her forehead, she'd continued, so that there would be
no room for misunderstanding, 'God Almighty has given
enough to Transport Cheemas of Sialkot, and I neither
need nor prefer my daughter-in-law to do a job—any job,
even one not involving teaching unwomanly exercises in a
Christian school. It is only because you insist.'

Harpreet had given another nod to show that she
understood, and was about to speak, when her mother-
in-law hurried to add, 'But the salary is rather good.' She'd
been worried that the bride might take her objections
too seriously.

Manjeet had returned with tea and had sat down
quietly on the other side of his mother, not wanting to
interrupt the conversation. 'You want to come back to

your seat?' his mother had asked, sipping the tea noisily. But she'd continued to sit between the two of them without even a pretence of getting up. Harpreet had excused herself, murmuring something about washing her hands, and while squeezing past Manjeet, had tapped him hard on his shin with the edge of her sole. She'd returned in a few minutes and stood assertively in the aisle, waiting for them to move so that she could sit next to her husband. This game of musical chairs which had started in the first few hours of her wedding, had continued with only slight variations throughout the duration of the marriage.

~

As Firdaus turned the corner into the even narrower lane which led to her house, she saw a bangle-seller come out of the door, carrying dozens of brightly coloured glass bangles on a wooden stand which she rested on her shoulder like a cross. It was surprising, since both Bushra and her mother-in-law abhorred bangles, calling them a Hindu custom. Curiously, though dressed in a colourful ghagra-choli, the woman was not wearing the typical kolhapuri chappals, but a pair of black Bata shoes. She had hurriedly turned towards the other end of the lane and the two women did not pass each other. It was the time of the day when the men were away. As Firdaus entered her house with the burqa now folded on her arm, she found that the atmosphere in the courtyard was tense. Her mother-in-law seemed numb with shock. Bushra stuttered when agitated and it was a while before Firdaus could gather what had happened.

'Hey, is this your father's house, that you are marching in without permission?' her mother-in-law had shouted at the intruding stranger. In return, the bangle-seller had rolled her eyes up towards her colourful wares, and pleaded, 'Please buy some, auntie. I haven't sold any since morning.'

Firdaus' mother-in-law had told her curtly to get out of the house since nobody in the family wore bangles. The bangle-seller had instead put her bangle stand down and rested it against a wall, infuriating the old lady. Bushra had come running from the kitchen to see what was going on.

'I am in fact looking for an old customer, Harpreet Cheema, who is very fond of bangles. She used to live in Iqbal Chowk before and I am told that she now lives here,' the young woman in the exotic ghagra-choli covered with mirrorwork and incongruous black shoes had replied, her manner indicating that she would have welcomed at least a long talk, if the sale of bangles was not a possibility.

'Bibi, you are clearly mistaken. This is the house of Muslim Cheemas and everybody knows that all the Sikh Cheemas went to India more than a year ago, at the time of Partition,' Bushra had chimed in from the other end of courtyard.

'Now, you pick up that flashy piece of devilry and get out of our house,' blustered her mother.

The woman had left the courtyard in a huff, but not before turning back at the door and shouting, 'Everybody also knows that many Sikh and Hindu girls were abducted in the chaos of Partition and forced into conversion and marriage. And now that the government has woken up from slumber, it is payback time!'

After hearing the story, Firdaus was also disturbed, but tried to play it down, 'So what is the big deal? What is new? Everybody knows it and everybody knows it is true about me, too. What can a bangle-seller do anyway? And how can a marriage be undone? There's no point in stewing over every wandering person's remarks. Let's eat, please.'

~

She sat on the cot in the veranda, eating mutton korma and rice with relish, as the hockey and exercise sessions with her students made her very hungry around this time of the day. But the bangle-seller had raked up things not too deeply buried. It was in this very veranda and on this very cot that she had regained consciousness, early one morning, to find her hands tied and forehead bleeding. Strange faces had looked down at her, as if she were an animal in a zoo.

For weeks before that, Sialkot, like all North Indian cities at the time, had been fast slipping into anarchy. Half the shops in the city—those belonging to Hindus and Sikhs—had been torched by mobs. Men were openly stabbed in the street by cheering squads. Houses were attacked and women carried away. Police stations, if approached, were found locked.

Harpreet did remember waking up in her own house earlier that night. It was full of flames and acrid smoke. Manjeet and his mother were nowhere around. The house was almost empty, since Manjeet had been busy shifting boxes, furniture and even clothes to his sister's house in Gurdaspur, which was likely to be on the Indian side of the future border. He had used his bus, which plied between Sialkot and Gurdaspur, to shift his household goods, bit by bit. In fact, the three of them had planned to slip away on it, the very next morning. The bus was parked just around the corner, in readiness for the journey. Earlier, sitting in the staff room next to the chapel at the school, it had taken her an hour to write the three lines of her resignation since she could not stop crying. Her job was her only regret about going away. When she had gone to the Principal's office to say farewell, she had started crying all over again, as she pulled herself away from Sister Agnes' embrace.

She remembered clawing and kicking at a tall man… had he been trying to pick her up and carry her away? There had been many other men, going from one smoke-filled room to the other, picking up a radio here, a watch there, cursing that there was not much left. Harpreet had coughed and spluttered because of the smoke, worrying all the while about what could have become of her husband and mother-in-law. She'd slipped once again from the grip of the insistent man and run out of the bedroom through a door which was now framed in flame. Then, there had been a searing pain on the side of her head and she had passed out, only to find herself bound and bleeding in this circle of strange faces.

'Why have you brought this woman here, Murtaza?' an old lady was asking in a pointed manner, glaring at a vaguely familiar looking tall young man across Harpreet's head.

'Ma, I want to get married to her. I have seen her pass in front of our factory,' he said, as if that was reason enough for abducting a woman. But, if the sheer frivolity of his reasoning process had been pointed out, Murtaza would have reeled off the names of several friends, relatives and acquaintances, all respectable people, who had done just that for almost the same reason.

Harpreet was conscious now but her mind was so full of a sickening worry about her husband and mother-in-law that she could not fully comprehend the import of the conversation. Besides, she did not remember seeing any factory on her way to the convent.

'But she is not a Muslim,' the argument continued above her.

'She will convert. She will qubool Islam,' Murtaza asserted. It was the way he had heard it was supposed to happen.

Bushra, Murtaza's wife, had decided at this point that enough was enough, 'Murtaza Cheema, Islam allows you four marriages but nowhere is it written that you will roast in hellfire if you do not marry four times. Besides, the world will spit on your face if you have two wives and your brother, just two years younger, has none. If another marriage has to happen in this house, it should be his.'

Just then, another man, even taller than Murtaza, but with a boyish face, had come ambling out from the house, clearly surprised to see that the cause of the commotion which had disturbed his sleep was a gaggle of neighbours surrounding an injured girl lying on a cot. Bushra had taken him aside to bring him up to date, with much whispering and gesticulation.

'Aslam, look what Murtaza has done,' his mother, clearly distraught and far less tactful than Bushra, had shouted across the courtyard.

Aslam had, albeit with folded hands, shooed the neighbours away to go mind their own business. They had scurried out, disappointed at being cut out of the excitement. Next, he'd asked Bushra to get him water and a clean cloth and had cleaned the cut on Harpreet's forehead, gently.

'Who else was there in the house with you?' he'd asked Harpreet in a crisp tone, as if she was the one who had barged into their house, while freeing her from the cot's rough ropes.

'My husband and mother-in-law… but I could not see them when he burnt our house.' She'd looked accusingly at the uncouth Murtaza.

'I did not burn the house. It was already up in roaring flames, when I reached. There was a crowd. But I saw her husband and mother-in-law run out of the house.

Somebody said they drove away in a bus parked in the lane. I rescued her. If I had not carried her away, the mob would have killed her. I brought her here in a tonga. He charged three rupees.' Murtaza had replied, pluming himself a little on his apparently altruistic conduct in front of his younger brother.

Harpreet had stood up and said that the first thing she wanted to do was to get out of that house and go to the police.

'But I already paid the sub-inspect–' Murtaza stopped short, correctly surmising that his earlier story of rescuing a girl from a burning house out of the sheer goodness of his heart would no longer hold any water. Aslam turned away from him, put on his shoes, and in a deceptively quiet voice, asked Bushra to lend her chappals and a dupatta to the Sikh girl. 'Let us go to the police,' he told her, gently.

The police post was next to the cigarette shop where the two lanes crossed. There were three spartan rooms and a small courtyard. The sub-inspector had seen the girl lying in the back of the tonga last night, when Murtaza had stopped here to give him forty rupees. Reflecting that in any case no one would demand them back from him, he wrote down her account faithfully on a loose sheet of paper and put it in an already half-full drawer. 'You can stay here, if you want, till we find another place for you,' he offered generously. Harpreet looked around the courtyard. A Primus stove and unwashed utensils were lying in one corner and the plume and feathers of a chicken in the other. She shuddered and said to Aslam, 'I want to go to my house and have a look.'

The street in front of the house was wet and slippery. The neighbours had hosed water from their roofs to stop the fire from spreading to their own houses, and it had eventually burnt itself out. Of the house, only a charred shell was left, and some of it had already collapsed.

Harpreet had walked past the house till she could see the end of the lane and the banyan tree where the bus used to be parked. The void under the tree had hit her like a wallop. She'd sunk down onto the brick platform under the tree, as her mind tried to absorb the full impact of what had happened.

She was alone and had nothing of her own. Not even the country she was in. It felt strange to think that she had been abandoned. She tried to tell herself that Manjeet could not have come back to get her without being killed himself, but it made no difference.

She didn't know how long she'd sat there, unmoving. At one point she'd got to her feet with a start when she saw a girl in school uniform walk past the mouth of the lane. Then she'd remembered that she had resigned from the school, and slumped back down.

Back at Aslam's house, she'd asked if she could sleep somewhere. Aslam had unlocked the door of a storeroom in the courtyard. The room was filled with brand-new, deflated footballs, covering the floor and reaching up to her knees. Aslam had picked up some that had tumbled out and thrown them back into the room. 'We make footballs. The workshop has no space, so we use this room to store them, but I will remove these and put in a cot.' Aslam had explained.

Harpreet had told him not to bother. For the next month, she had slept on the firm yet yielding bed of airless footballs bound for Spain and Portugal.

Her lunch completed, Firdaus walked to the hand pump and washed her plate. During that first month, she had gone several times to the central post office and to the main police station to see if there was something for her. There was nothing, then or later.

At the end of the month, Harpreet consented for her name to be changed to Firdaus and said 'qubool hai' to the maulvi who asked if she was willing for a nikah to Aslam Cheema for a mahr of one thousand rupees.

The next morning, Firdaus had gone to the Convent and applied for her old job. The nuns had been delighted to have her back. It was true that her certificates carried a different name, but that had been sorted out after the Mother Superior herself certified that she knew from personal knowledge that Harpreet and Firdaus were the same person. She had also been handed a letter from her uncle in Jullundur, giving her the news that her father had died on the way to hospital after a heart attack, two weeks ago.

Aslam had said he understood when she decided that

she wanted to keep sleeping in the room of footballs for some more time.

The year and a half after that was a happy time in the life of Firdaus Cheema. She liked her work. The Sisters at the convent loved her vivacity and learnt how to play volleyball from her. Aslam gifted them the net and volleyballs. He even fixed the poles and lights at his own expense. It was true that Bushra was sometimes jealous of her because she had often seen Murtaza look at Firdaus as if she was something edible. And their mother-in-law was full of praise for her for working 'like a man'.

~

When Aslam came home and was told about the bangle-seller, he looked troubled and decided to find out if there was anything to it. Aslam and Firdaus went out on his motorcycle to the house of Farukh, a police inspector and Aslam's distant cousin. Farukh was not home, but came shortly, chewing a paan. He told them that the bangle-seller was in all likelihood a worker from a non-profit organization which had been roped in by the government to locate Hindu women left behind during the chaos of Partition.

'But why now?' Aslam asked.

Farukh knew all about this since he had just returned from Lahore after attending a two-day workshop on the 'Special Campaign for Repatriation of Hindu Women'. 'Because now the two governments have reached an agreement to return thousands of such women on both sides to their parent countries,' he said as if reading out from a government pamphlet.

'Firdaus here has accepted Islam and is married to me.' Aslam was clearly perplexed at the suggestion that the wheels of time could indeed be turned back.

'The agreement between India and Pakistan says that all the religious conversions and subsequent marriages of women which happened after 1st March, 1947, on both sides, are cancelled.'

'Cancelled? How can anybody cancel my marriage?' Firdaus almost shouted.

Farukh rummaged through a drawer and came up with some of the documents that had been distributed at the workshop, 'Look here. This is a copy of the agreement. See here at point two.'

They read: 'Conversion of persons abducted after 1st March, 1947 will not be recognized, and all such persons must be restored to their respective Dominions. The wishes of the persons concerned are irrelevant. Consequently, recording the statements of such persons before magistrates is not necessary.'

Farukh tried to tell his cousin what a lawyer at the workshop had told the participants: 'The two countries are taking the whole issue as a matter of their country's honour. They have made a new law on each side. It is called the "Abducted Persons' Recovery and Restoration Act".'

'Honour! My foot! Where were the countries when my house was burnt? When my family was made to flee and

I was carried away like a sack of potatoes by a man who lusted for me? I appealed to the government then. Nobody gave a damn about my honour. Why should I give a damn about any country's honour? Don't I have any opinion about whether I want to go back or not? If I say that I am happy where I am, and nobody is forcing me to stay and that I have a job here which I rather like, does that have no meaning?'

Farukh's wife, who had brought tea, sat next to Firdaus and pressed her hand gently. Aslam, who had been biting his lip, asked, 'Tell me Farukh! In the last one and a half years, I have never seen the Pakistan government be so focussed in anything they have done so far. Why now?'

'Because there is an immense pressure from families on this side to get back the thousands of Muslim women living with Hindu men on the other side. Those women cannot come back till the thousands of Hindu women living here are returned. It is a quid pro quo. Add the honour of the two countries and you have your reason for urgency. They have swept all pending issues aside—God knows are plenty of those! In fact, the campaign is already well on its way.

'So far, the local police had been openly hostile to the campaign. So the government is now offering cash incentives: two hundred rupees for each woman recovered. And they have appointed liaison officers in each district to locate such women with the help of voluntary outfits. Their workers roam the streets dressed as itinerant vendors—like your bangle-seller.'

'Is there anything at all that we can do?' Aslam asked Farukh.

'Go to Bhimber for some time and hope that this blows over. It is just an hour away on your motorcycle,' Farukh advised.

'Why Bhimber? Isn't Bhimber in Pakistan?' Aslam asked.

'No, technically it isn't. It is in Azad Kashmir. And the agreement was between India and Pakistan, not between India and Azad Kashmir. You will find other couples there, waiting for things to cool down.'

In the lane outside, while they were walking towards the motorcycle, a rubber ball came flying towards Firdaus. She caught it expertly. Young boys were playing pitthoo. A pudgy boy who reminded her of Manjeet had tried to hit the clay shards placed one upon another, and missed. Harpreet threw the ball in one precise, angry movement. The clay shards shattered into smithereens, chips flying all over the lane.

* * *

Harpreet woke up groggy, surprised to find herself in a hospital bed with a needle stuck to her arm. Her eyes followed the tube connecting it to a bottle hanging upside down from a stand next to her bed. There was a sore feeling, not in her stomach, but deeper, close to where she had cramps during her periods. Why was she here? After a painful effort, she recollected that she had been brought to a place which looked like a hostel, from Sialkot, three days ago. She'd been in a bus full of noisy women, with a police jeep in front of the bus and another behind. There was a short stop at the border, and then Indian police jeeps had taken over. Harpreet had sat on the last seat and remembered that when she last crossed this place, the border was not there. She played in her mind with this conundrum. Where had the border been when she crossed it last time? It didn't exist...but then how could she have crossed it?

She'd watched the women in the bus, remembering her return to Sialkot with Aslam, after spending a month and a half in a cramped hotel room in hot and dusty Bhimber. A pompous government officer had been waiting for them in the courtyard, with two women—one of them the bangle-seller in the Bata shoes—and four policemen. Probably Bushra had had something to do with the perfect timing; she was suspiciously smooth-faced and silent, compared to the shocked anger and protests of Murtaza and his mother.

Firdaus had clung to Aslam and refused to let go. Aslam had eventually gently prised her grip loose himself. She had looked at him and asked, 'When I asked you once how come both of us are Cheemas, you had replied that our ancestors, before they became Sikh or Muslim, were a quarrelsome, fighter tribe.'

Aslam had nodded.

'So, why don't we fight?'

'Harpreet,' he had said, not Firdaus, 'Nobody can fight destiny, not even Cheemas.'

She'd noticed that the women in the bus from Sialkot were an odd mix. Some looked relieved, others fearful, and still others, lost. And each woman was a strange mix within herself. During the journey, the same woman who said she was joyous about going to India, would start crying hysterically and wanting to get off the bus, to head back to Pakistan. It was a bus full of mad women, she'd thought dully.

The bus from Sialkot had finally stopped near Jullunder, at this large hostel-like building, which seemed to be full, judging by the amount of chatter coming from the dining room, of young women. A sprinkling of older women in doctors' coats were walking busily around. Harpreet had been told that her husband, Manjeet Singh Cheema, who had given her name to the government for repatriation, would come after three days to fetch her after the paperwork was complete. Meanwhile, she would be seen by the doctors for a routine medical clearance.

She'd wondered why she should need any medical clearance. The first question the doctor had asked her was about the time of her last periods, which had been before they had gone to Bhimber. But like most women athletes, her periods had always been irregular, she told the doctor.

She dozed off again. When she opened her eyes, a woman in her late thirties wearing a white, embroidered sari was sitting in a chair next to her bed.

'I am Miss Sarabhai. You can call me Mridula. How are you feeling now?'

'What have they done to me? I feel sore.'

'Didn't they tell you? You were a few weeks pregnant. They did a little procedure. You are fine to go home now.'

Harpreet was so taken aback that she sat up abruptly. The cannula attached to her arm came off and the fluid spurted onto Miss Sarabhai's sari. Dark blood came dribbling out of other end of the needle which was still stuck in Harpreet's arm. A nurse who saw this rushed to take the needle out from her arm.

'But nobody said anything to me!' Harpreet realized she was crying, her hands clutching the sheets. 'How could they decide that I did not want to have the baby?' her voice had become louder. A woman on the next bed woke up from the anaesthesia and started moaning in pain.

Miss Sarabhai said, 'I hate the way they do this thing, but when the families ask for repatriation, the protocol includes consent for abortion. Because this is the way the families want it to be. I have seen hundreds of them. Nobody ever wanted to have a woman back who was pregnant. The husbands say that if Ram wanted Sita to be pristine pure when she was brought back from Lanka, an ordinary man has at least a right to insist that his wife is not pregnant from another man. So, the state is doing what the families want. They have allocated a special fund just for this.'

'Let them not have me back! Am I a possession which can be dragged anywhere and then cut up to throw away parts of me which they don't like?' Harpreet shouted, in between sobs. What had they done to her? An abortion.

The word struck her. 'And isn't abortion illegal for God's sake?' she asked fiercely.

Miss Sarabhai said weakly, 'When the state undertakes such missions, maybe it is not.'

Three hours later she was in a hall full of women. Some sort of briefing was going on. Some of them were to go to the waiting hall near the reception, where somebody from their 'family' was already waiting. They read a list of names, and she heard hers among them. The rest were to exit from the side door and a blue bus would be waiting in the parking lot to take them to a specially set-up reception centre in Delhi. Women milled around and the buzz of voices was deafening after the silence for the announcement.

On her way out, Harpreet went to the bathroom and looked at the fatigue lines on her face. She washed her face with soap and felt a little better. From her handbag, she took out a lipstick and took her time applying it. She thought that her nails were looking chipped. She used a file to even the edges and applied nail polish from a tiny bottle with Urdu markings. Satisfied with her handiwork, she carefully took off from her neck and wrists the religious amulets that she had collected over time, from both sides. Without any qualms, she flushed these down the lavatory, and strode out of the building.

In the parking lot, there was a yellow bus with the inscription, 'Cheema Transport Company' and, closer to her, a blue one, which had already started moving. Harpreet held up her hand. The driver braked and asked when she was inside, 'Dilli?'

She nodded.

When the conductor came to her seat with his clipboard and asked her name, she replied, 'Harpreet.'

The bus conductor, who was just a boy with the first fuzz of a moustache, asked, 'Just Harpreet? Agge pichhe kuchh nahi? Nothing before or after?'

She smiled at him and said, 'Agge pichhe kuchh nahi.'

THE DIARY OF A MENTAL
HOSPITAL INTERN

Sunita, the department clerk, handed over a letter posting me to the mental hospital in Ranchi for two months. Starting 1st November. A week from tomorrow. I knew it was coming; it's part of the training, but there is hardly any time. Must book a train ticket. And it is a two-night journey.

'Residents are supernumerary these months. Good time to go,' says Sunita.

Hangover: 7.3 on Richter. See-off party by the residents last night. Everybody drank as if I was going to the border. Packed books, some woollens for December, borrowed money (Kalka–Howrah Mail, only second-class ticket available, not third). Parting talk by Professor: 'Be good. Bring laurels.' Leaving tomorrow night.

2 a.m. Alighted at Gaya. 'Budhha had his enlightenment here. I will get mine at Ranchi', thought sleepily, suitcase in hand, trying to avoid the sleeping dogs. Shared the taxi with three others. Undulating landscape, then low hills, a tucked-away city. Drizzling, cool, balmy. Basic hostel. Awesome omelettes. Love the place.

Will spend first month at the European Hospital and second at the Indian. Both made by the British—didn't want their countrymen to mingle with Indians in so vulnerable a condition as mental illness. Is there another example of apartheid among the mentally ill anywhere else in the world? I do not know.

Sprawling campus. Two hundred rolling acres. A huge gate dwarfs everyone; most use the smaller in-built door. The main gate opens only when the Super's motor or the supply trucks have to pass. Sixteen wards, separated by acres of fields. The semi-arid soil has been made fertile through forced hard work by generations of mentally ill patients, packaged as occupational therapy. To go from the first to the last ward, one needs at least a bicycle. Hired one from the cycle repair shop under the banyan.

Wherever you go, a patient's gaze follows you. Anybody new could have—just possibly may have—come to take him home. Will meet the Super tomorrow. Today is a local holiday.

2nd November

The Super likes to talk. Armchair psychiatry is what is taught in Institutes. This here is the real karmabhoomi, where work is worship. Unlearn some things to make space. Study files, speak to patients. Concentrate on the individual. There are no relatives anyway.

7th November

Met patients who have been here for decades, since before Independence, including many old British men and women. Departing rulers simply forgot to take them along. Spent hours with dog-eared files in semi-dark record rooms. Electricity is erratic. Long histories and 'progress' notes, of persons who have spent half their lives here and will die here.

13th November

Even the Indian patients are more or less abandoned. The families simply left them here and did not come back, even when the hospital wrote to say that their wards had recovered. Stacks of sent letters with the red stamps of the Returned Letters Office lie in a heap in a corner, tied with jute string. Families found that it was more convenient to live without the patient. The longer the person stayed away, the more the family did not want him back. Often someone else—brother, sister, uncle—usurped the man's property, so the last thing they want is the legal owner to turn up.

'So much for The Great Indian Family and its protective nurturing,' quipped the pipe-smoking former manager of a tea plantation in Siliguri, whom I initially thought was a visitor, looking at the piles of returned letters.

25th November

Have still not seen the whole campus. The cycle chain broke. Don't want to hire another cycle, just for five days, so am taking long walks to the wards during the afternoons. Waylaid by an abrupt shower while on the women's side— sprinted to the nearest building, which turns out to be the Anna Freud Ward. Sigmund Freud has a ward named after him on the men's side.

It's a 'halfway home' for women who have recovered, at least partially. Built like a house, with a sitting room, a lobby, a dining room and bedrooms upstairs. The best-kept place on campus. 'Residents' wear their own clothes, not uniforms. Are free to go out. Actual table-cloths and real flowers on the hall table in the lobby. All tastefully done. Had a feeling that I was trespassing.

'Can I help you?' says a shadow from a table in the corner. Dark clouds have muffled the sunlight, indoor lights not switched on yet. Somebody is smoking. An attractive, middle-aged, apparently English woman. Only, the features, a little too sharp and delicate. She stands up and introduces herself, 'Nicole Forrester'. I notice the sari, the copper hair, the bindi, a tentative spot of sindoor and the Wills Filters.

'Care for a smoke?' she asks. Took one from the packet held out by her. 'Aren't you the new doctor from up north who has come to see first-hand how awful the conditions are in mental hospitals?' Nicole wants to know with an arched eyebrow and a mocking tone.

'Yes, I am Prakash Kohli from Chandigarh,' I say, letting the banter go by the board. Do not be patronizing, I had been advised, 'I am just a trainee, here to learn long-term care. Do you work here?'

'Yes, I do work here now, but I started as a patient, which I continue to be. I am on treatment for schizophrenia,' Nicole says, hands clasped behind her head, the cigarette smouldering in the ash tray we are sharing. I should not be sitting here smoking with a patient, the thought crosses my mind, and I imagine the scowl on Professor's face, adjusting his glasses to read again, in my report from the Super, the bit about smoking with white women, underlined in red.

As if reading my thoughts, Nicole reassures me, 'Relax doctor, it is fine. I am a regular staff member too. I get paid. Besides, my husband was a psychiatrist in this very hospital,' she says wryly.

The downpour is heavier now. For the next hour, sitting in the semi dark lobby of a house-like hospital ward, I listen to the story of Nicole Forrester in her soft voice, against the background pitter-patter on the sloping roof. She talks haltingly, as if she thinks in French and speaks in English, substituting a Hindi word when she can't get the right English one.

'I was born after the end of the First World War, in a coastal village, on the French Riviera, near Nice. My parents were doctors and wanted me to be one. Not knowing whether to obey or defy them and not knowing what I wanted to do with myself, I trained as a nurse and then worked in a hospital in Marseilles for a year. But I soon got tired of caring for sailors sick with gonorrhoea, and stitching wounds from drunken brawls. An opening came up in a small hospital in Paris and I moved. There, I met Peter Forrester, an English doctor touring France. Peter wanted to work with psychiatric patients. In those days, places where you could get a formal training in psychiatry were very rare, even in Europe. There was a possibility that if he were to move to India, he could get employment in a psychiatric hospital, which was affiliated to the University of London for its diploma course.'

Nicole gets up to open a window and let out the smoke. She is barefoot and I cannot help looking at the tribal toe-ring with a tiny fish against the pale translucent skin. 'Hitler had already invaded Poland. Before either France or England got involved, we left France and, after spending a week with Peter's parents, got married. With the German attack on France imminent any day, my parents could not come. After a week of paperwork in London, we sailed for Calcutta. On the ship, I taught Peter some French and learnt some English—and some Cockney slang.' Nicole has an alluring smile.

'The six years that we spent in one of the bigger houses just outside the hospital were the happy times,' she says, blowing a perfect ring. 'Twice a month we would take a train to Calcutta to attend exuberant parties thrown by the homesick British. Calcutta during the forties was a hep city, famous for those bashes.' Her voice was now low, and she was increasingly indifferent about recalling exact English words, and would let out a French word or two, rather than make the effort. 'Some of the later trips to Calcutta were for medical investigations since I was unable to conceive.'

'It was in the winter of 1942 that we received the news of my parents' death.' Nicole pulls out a cigarette, looks at it as if she did not recognize what it was, and then puts it back . 'A random strafing by a German aircraft out after the Resistance, killed both of them in their car. The cable had been sent by my aunt. She was the only relative I now had. It was very unsafe to travel to France in those days. In any case, it took weeks for the news to reach me; the burial would have taken place.' Feeling chilly, she pulls her feet under her chair.

'Trips to Calcutta...*devenaient de plus en plus frustrant*. I was finding it difficult to cope with travelling, and with cycles of investigations and procedures. Waiting every month, only to face emptiness was telling on both of us and the idea of adoption was already hovering in the... *contexte*.'

More and more French was being thrown in, as she could not find substitutes. I must have looked perplexed and she apologizes, '*Désolé*', looking rather forlorn, but for just a few moments, 'Let me try and do better.'

'In the summer of '46, Peter had high fever, which was diagnosed as a particularly virulent form of malaria. He was in coma for six weeks at the Ranchi General Hospital. He died, not of malaria, but of cardiac arrest brought on by too much quinine, early one morning.' Her arm is covering her eyes, her head resting on the back of the easy chair. I do not think she is crying, but she does not speak for some time.

'That was when I went loco,' Nicole says at last, with a sense of relief, as if she has just finished a painful climb uphill. She gets up to switch on the lights. Three cigarette butts are crushed in the ashtray, two with faint lipstick marks. 'For three months, I had to be given injections to sleep. I kept on hearing Peter's voice, but as if he was talking to somebody else about me, and not to me. Nice things, like how much he loved me. I tried to talk to him but it was like he didn't hear me and would go on talking about me. It was very, very...frustrating. I started running out in the rain in my nightclothes. I was admitted here in this very ward. It was a proper ward then. They diagnosed me with schizophrenia.

'Peter's parents came. They offered to take me with them, but I was in no position to travel. They wrote later, asking me to come and live with them. By then, I just did not want to go anywhere at all. There was nobody left in France for me. My aunt, too, had died a year after my parents' death. Here, everybody knew me. People cared for me.'

'So, I just stayed back, even after the management changed in this country,' she smiles. 'I recovered slowly.

And here I am. No regrets twenty-five years later. I enjoy my work. When you have been on both sides of the table, you get an intriguing third perspective. The weather is nice. Most of the time, I am well. I have to take a depot injection every month, otherwise the voices come back. The doctors prescribe it and I inject myself. They get it from abroad, I am told.'

Nicole puts the matchbox at the edge of the table and flicks it with her nail. It lands on my side of the table. She asks, 'What does the brilliant North Indian psychiatrist think about my case?' The mocking tone is back. Looking at the graceful lines on her face, I flick the matchbox back to her side, and mimicking her mocking tone, say, 'Well, the North Indian psychiatrist does not have to be particularly brilliant to make out that you are normal now. I think that the illness, whatever it was, left you years back, but you are clutching its leftovers. You are not letting go of it because this is the only way you can hear his voice.'

She looks taken aback and for the first time there is a tinge of irritation in her voice, as she says, '*Oui*...you may be right. But I do not want to forget him.'

'Personally, I do think, it would be better if you could grapple with the voices, once and for all. Because, let's face it, it's not actually his voice. Do you watch Hindi movies?'

'Yes. They are cute.'

'If you choose to let go and say goodbye—a real, agonizing, heart-rending, earth-shattering, sindoor-wiping goodbye—with a little help from your doctor, then, maybe after a while you would not need the shots. But mind you, what I offer is only an opinion, and not so well informed at that. I am just a trainee. Your psychiatrist would know better.'

'And my schizophrenia?' she asks.

'If you are schizophrenic, then I am Chinese,' I reply honestly, looking straight into those azure, aging eyes.

She says it is the nicest thing that anybody has said to her in years.

'But I do think that anybody, who chooses to stay in landlocked Ranchi, when the other option is the French Riviera, has to be a little crazy after all.'

1st December

This month I'm at the 'Indian Hospital', run by the state government and just a mile away from its richer 'European' cousin, which is funded by the central government. I went to meet the director, Dr Lokesh Varma, at seven-thirty. The sun is quite high up already by this time, here in the east. The office is always chock-full of people, their expressions varying from detached nonchalance to mortal fear. Many more wait outside, around the tea-shop. Highly disturbed psychotics and their relatives.

A dishevelled man with matted hair was being helped out of an auto-rickshaw by a ten-year-old boy, apparently his son. His hands were tied with a rope, the child holding the other end. When the son found that they would have to wait, he expertly tied his end of rope to a tree and settled down to wait patiently on his haunches. It seemed as if he had done it several times before.

Dr Varma was fiftyish, greying and athletic. Apart from him, there was only one other doctor, a middle-aged man in thick glasses. When Varma saw me enter, he guessed who I was and quietly waved me to take a chair and start seeing patients. He pushed a stack of blank files towards me, and we set to work without exchanging a word. He was just happy to have another doctor. When I fumbled for anything—a pen, more paper—he would slide whatever I needed to me.

We worked till eight in the evening. The canteen served lunch and tea and the three of us ate in turns. Most patients were either excited or in a stupor, refusing medicines and food, and had to be admitted. Varma saw the man with the matted hair, and I didn't catch the diagnosis, but he joined the patients admitted to the hospital. A nurse took the rope from the child and the man was led away towards the inner gate. The boy stood lost for a moment, and then quietly walked out.

14th December

Have been working in the OPD from eight to eight, including Sundays. Have never seen so many people with mental illness at one place. Varma is a non-verbal man. Talks in monosyllables. But not gruff. Had a teaching job in London at King's College, nurses tell me. Came here five years ago, after his divorce. One twelve-year-old son, in hostel. That's all that is known about him. The other doctor changes each day, rotating from the wards.

It's as if there is a huge factory out there, producing madness. People are brought in droves, from as far away as the Nepal, Bhutan and Burma borders. Auto-rickshaws are perpetually unloading psychotics in the courtyard outside the office. If they arrive at night, they wait under the banyan tree till the teashop gets going at seven in the morning and the clinic opens. There is only one way to examine large numbers of highly disturbed patients twelve hours a day. Focus on the symptoms—violence, not eating, not sleeping, lying stiff like a board for days—not the causes, which could be anything or nothing. No way to tell without intensive observation. Keeps you sane—there is no time for more anyway. Hopefully somebody in the wards looks at them as individuals.

Varma spoke to me for the first time about my assignment, in two staccato bursts: 'Spend the remaining two weeks in the wards,' and 'By the way, you have a knack for severe mental illness.' Whatever that means. Made me very happy, though.

20th December

There are eighteen wards, twelve for men and six for women. Each ward is meant for forty persons but often has double that number. The extras sleep on straw mats on the floor between beds. One junior doctor supervises three wards. Each ward has a nurse with a cleaner to help. What the place does not lack is land. Sprawling ill-kempt lawns and fields, dotted with thousands of perennial, self-sustaining trees.

Several earthen oil lamps and loads of marigold flowers are lying between the roots of a banyan tree outside a male ward. Sheltered by the broad trunk, the flames were steadily leaf-shaped. Some sort of Purnima today, so no non-veg, not even omelettes, the cook said.

The ward is noisy, cramped and dirty. Around forty of the men are wearing hospital uniforms. Found out later that the other thirty men are also patients, in mufti. Uniforms, like beds, are only for the sanctioned number. Surrounded by the raucous crowd of semi-dressed, unshaven, excited restless men is Gracy Thomas, the ward nurse. Gracy is dark, painfully thin and frightfully young for the job. The white uniform is spotless and she wears a red bindi. She is sweeping the floor with a broom, as the sweepers are on strike.

I am told to sit in her chair and wait till she cleans. While I look at the files, she sweeps the ward and then makes up the beds. She knows each patient by name. Highly agitated men silently obey the frail young girl.

Rubbing her hands in a satisfied manner, Gracy comes to the table. 'I am from Kerala', she says, picking up a cardboard box full of tiny envelopes in which she has put the morning medication for each patient, each labelled in a neat unhurried handwriting. She goes to each bed with one envelope and a glass of water from the water cooler. An experienced nurse, she makes them open their mouths afterwards, checking to see that the medicine has been swallowed. She seems to crack jokes as she goes along. Patients smile at her. For the men on mattresses she has to kneel on the floor. It takes her an hour. When I offer to help, she says, 'You will make mistakes.'

'You speak good Hindi,' I say when she comes back.

'I do not speak Hindi,' she informs me unwinkingly.

'Come on, you were joking with them. They were laughing.'

'Oh, that. I joke in Malayalam. They laugh in Hindi.' I thought for a moment that she was pulling my leg. She was not. 'I understand them. They understand me.'

21st December

Went to the female side of the hospital, which, it turns out, is on the other side of the highway. One has to wait at the traffic lights to cross. The breakfast queues are long but disciplined. Saima Bhatti, the matron runs a tight ship. She happens to be from Gurdaspur and is delighted to be able to speak Punjabi with somebody.

As we go on the rounds, we pass a twenty-something girl in a loose grey dress, being held by a woman warden while a boyish barber with a beedi stuck behind his ear crops her long tresses. The girl looks at me with eyes brimming with tears.

'This is a new admission,' Saima tells me. Cropping of hair is compulsory. 'It is a matter of hygiene,' she says. I say maybe it should also be a matter of choice, and they should wait to see if the girl can take care of herself. The Punjabi camaraderie goes sour and after a double-quick round of the premises, I and the barber, now finished with his job, are promptly escorted back to the traffic lights by a frosty Saima Bhatti herself. She actually waits till we cross, making sure I don't come back.

22nd December

I think Saima complained, and I am now being treated as a subversive human-rights activist and not merely an extra pair of benign hands. I have a minder now, Jugnu, a peon from the superintendent's office. He's a bouncy, cheerful boy, who happily takes me around all the male wards. Gives a wide grin, shaking his head, as if to a naughty child, when I suggest we cross the road to Saima Bhatti's bastion. I am also told that my assignment will finish a week early, the day after tomorrow, since there's only a skeletal staff and nobody to help me during the winter break.

24th December

My last day in Ranchi. Visited the farthest ward, after which there was only the concrete wall, topped with shards of glass and rolls of barbed-wire fencing. There, I meet Panditji, tall and wiry, with a bald head and dark leathery skin, the result of time spent outdoors, gardening.

Was surprised to hear that Panditji is a patient and not one of the twenty-five gardeners, even though he works more than all of them put together. Lives in a small hut, which he has fabricated from jute and bamboo in the middle of a small garden that he has planted himself. The patch of land, just outside his ostensible ward, is a riot of colour, crowded with marigolds, chrysanthemums, roses of three different hues and many other flowers which I have never seen. Marigold plants are entangled in rose bushes and deep purple petunias wrapped around lily stems.

On seeing me come out of the ward, he spreads a mat in front of his hut. Panditji, it soon transpires, was admitted at the age of eighteen to Mental Hospital, Lahore. The first thing that comes to my mind is that he must have travelled with Rulda.

His father, a clerk in the Imperial Bank, had been promoted and transferred from Delhi to the bank's Lahore branch. He was a widower, said Panditji, and was at quite a loss when his only child was sent back from school burning with fever and babbling incoherently. The bank's doctor wrote a referral to Lahore Mental Hospital, and Anil Pandey was admitted, for what the father believed was an observation period of two weeks.

'Twenty-five years later, I am still here, although in another hospital and in a different country. My father died of injuries during the thick of the rioting, stabbed by a man who was paid seventy-five rupees to do it. It was passed off as a "Partition killing". A distant uncle who came from Agra when my father died told me when he visited me in the hospital that it was actually a jealous colleague who was superseded by my father.... A lot of that happened too,' Panditji continued, chewing on a grass-shoot, 'which nobody talks about, because it chips away some of the glamour from Partition. I mean, normal life, including mundane crime, could not have completely stopped during Partition.'

'My father's gratuity is still lying somewhere with the State Bank of Pakistan, because State Bank of India, the other twin child of Imperial Bank, did not claim it from its counterpart.'

The illness evolved as a manic depressive disorder over the years. 'Even now, in spite of taking lithium, Jugnu here knows that sometimes I do not come out of the hut for days, not even to water the plants. The matron sends over medicines and food. But at least I no longer go running around naked now.' Jugnu had quietly disappeared at five, when his duty finished.

I asked him about the exchange of the patients. 'They shifted the Indian patients, which just meant all the Hindus and Sikhs, to Amritsar in 1950. The Amritsar people kept the Punjabis and sent the rest of us to this place by a train which took two days to reach.'

'A woman jumped off when the train was crossing the Kosi River; she dropped a hundred feet down into sand and started running, unhurt. The train was stopped and it took two hours for the guards to catch up with her and bring her back up, kicking and screaming. She was given ECT in her coach, with a portable machine.'

Did Panditji know Rulda Singh or Fattu while in Lahore? Panditji tried to remember but gave up, 'I do not think so. It was like a small town, with so many different wards. Each ward was a separate world. And it was a long time back.'

I told him that in exchange for the Indian patients sent from Pakistan, 233 Muslim patients gathered from India were sent to Pakistan, in the same train which had brought him to Amritsar. Panditji already knew that. 'We saw those guys in the parallel queue at Attari railway station. They did not look too joyous, is all that I remember. But then, we were hardly bursting with happiness. A mental hospital is a mental hospital. Changing the country outside does not change much. I guess we all knew that.'

'Do you know if some patients were sent from here?'

'Yes, fifty went from Ranchi. The clerk told me. They were gone when we reached here. Others must have gone from mental hospitals in Uttar Pradesh. The clerk said it was a retarded thing to do. Just because a diplomat wrote in a file that some Muslim patients should be sent as a return gesture, people were picked up at random. Many of them did not understand Pakistan or India or freedom and the only Jinnah they probably knew was the occupational therapist; how could they tell if they wanted to go to Pakistan or not? And some who should have actually gone to Dhaka went to Lahore. The clerks looked at the names and said, 'Here is a Muslim for Lahore.' Nobody bothered about the fact that the fellow actually spoke Bengali, whenever he chose to speak, that is. Just because I was a Hindu but not a Punjabi, I was sent from Amritsar to Ranchi. Nobody checked that my home town was Agra!

'And once they were stamped to go to Pakistan, nobody bothered much about them. Partly because their journey was fixed and cancelled so many times in three years, they were considered as not belonging to the hospital and treated as step-children. They were ninety-five to start with, according to the clerk.'

Nobody spoke for a long time.

'Why do they call you Panditji?'

'Many years ago, a patient was dying in this ward. A very old man from Nepal. He was conscious till the end. He knew that I was a Brahmin and wanted me to whisper a mantra into his ear for moksha. I did not know any such mantra, but whispered some words anyway. Since then, they call me Panditji, and summon me every time a patient is dying, even to the women's' side, day or night. I have even learnt a Sanskrit mantra. With three thousand of us here, there is always somebody dying.'

I got up to go. He plucked several blue flowers shaped like little bells and placed those in my palm, closing my fingers softly over the flowers.

Jugnu came running out of the trees, 'Panditji, ward number eight, jaldi.'

FOLIE À DEUX

I met you the day after I completed my three-year residency and became a psychiatrist. In the hot and muggy waiting room, I had to jostle with patients and relatives waiting to see me. I was not wearing my white coat because of the heat, and nobody would give me way to reach my own cabin.

'You will have to let me pass if you want me to see you,' I told the elderly woman with hair down till her hips, who was standing aimlessly in the doorway. You appeared around the corner, tall and embarrassed, carrying a glass of water. Very gently, you took the woman aside.

An hour later, you were narrating the history of your mother's illness in a methodical fashion to me, with only occasional prompting from the miniscule jottings scribbled on the margins of a newspaper during your travel to Chandigarh. Your account contained words like 'episode', 'remission' and 'delusion', indicating that you had been in hospitals before. You said that it was the third time your mother had fallen ill in this manner, rolling the red mauli thread tied around your wrist, which reminded me that it was Janmashtami.

The first attack came a year after your parents moved from Multan to Patiala during Partition, in 1948. There were no children yet. It had all started with a feeling of foreboding at night during a thunderstorm. She had become fearful and swore that she had heard the whisperings of a mob, growing louder and shriller, threatening to carve her to pieces. She also vividly 'saw' bearded 'mussalmans' wearing clothes drenched in blood, threatening to amputate her breasts. You narrated this matter-of-factly. Shrieking, she had run out into the rain. Your father and some neighbours found her a couple of hours later at the railway station, asking people about the train to Multan. You did not know any more about this attack, since you'd only heard about it from your father.

No treatment was taken—there was none to be had in that town back then. Your father had tried to console her, saying that there were hardly any Muslims left in Patiala. An exorcist mumbled some words and gave her leaves from a herb to keep under her pillow. She had recovered, slowly and fitfully, in three or four months.

'That local healer was a Muslim,' you told me, with a wry smile.

The second bout was out of the blue, five years ago. After twenty lucid and peaceful years, during which she not just safely bore and wisely brought up three children, but also stoically grieved over the loss of her husband in an accident. You remembered the second attack vividly. You had been seventeen at the time. On that morning, you and Om, a year younger, had coaxed and cajoled her to sit between the two of you in the rickshaw to go to the hospital, but she had kept trying to get down and run away from the marauding Muslim mobs only she could see chasing you. Chitra, your younger sister, was the only person following the rickshaw, on her cycle. You had seen your mother's red eyes and wide pupils and your heart had sunk, but you did not cry then or later, because you were the big sister.

She was admitted to the municipal hospital for a month, during which she recovered. When she recovered, she recovered all the way, as if nothing had ever happened. She preferred not to talk about it, out of embarrassment, because she could remember everything clearly and knew the absurdity of it all. 'It was as if there was another person sleeping inside her,' you said, your gaze following your mother who was being taken by the nurse to check her blood pressure. 'She also had this superstition that any mention of it might bring the nightmare back.'

You continued in a precise manner, now in English so that your mother would not understand, nervously touching your nose pin every few moments. Your mother had again become guarded and distrustful lately. She would complain about the servants stealing away her gold jewellery, piece by piece. One afternoon, she hit the cleaner, accusing her of theft. You had also got a bruise on the back of your hand when you'd tried to intervene. I could see the purple mark on your slim wrist even as you smiled indulgently at your mother, to reassure her that she was not being complained against.

A week after the illness started this time, she had begun hearing the frightful voices again—the blessed 'mussalmans' wanting to cut her to pieces were back. This time they also threatened to rape her daughters, 'since they have grown up nicely,' the voices leered. She would cringe and hide in corners, terrified for her whole family. You had decided to bring her to a psychiatrist yourself.

I reassured you, saying that such delusions could often be treated completely with the appropriate medicines. I admitted her to the hospital, and had the satisfaction of seeing your mother make a fast recovery under my care. In three weeks she was well enough to go home. Om stayed with her throughout, as you had to be with Chitra, but you visited every other day, and were quick to pick up all the details of the care and medication schedule. After her discharge, you sent me a thank-you postcard written in a tiny scrawl, the first of many that I would receive in the years to come.

~

Six months later, another postcard informed me that your mother had killed herself. At some point after her discharge from the hospital, she had stopped taking the medication, complaining that it made her constantly sleepy. But she had remained fine and you hadn't been able to convince her of the importance of taking the medicines. She wouldn't hear of coming to see me for a different medication that might not make her sleepy. Then, one night, a wedding procession wound its way through the neighbourhood, complete with marching band, dholwallahs and firecrackers at every street corner. She had woken up and started shouting that the 'mussalmans' were battering down the front door and shots were being fired.

In her terror, she ran around the house, with you and Om after her. Now convinced that her persecutors were chasing her and about to catch up with her, she ran screaming to the roof. Before you knew what was happening, she had climbed the parapet and jumped into the night—landing on the asphalt road, a few steps ahead of a baraat of colourfully dressed and bejewelled wedding guests dancing merrily.

You had used all the space on the postcard, despite the tiny scrawl. Even though the words overlapped, each was perfectly legible. Remembering the tall gritty girl I had seen in my waiting room, I wrote a condolence letter and dropped it off at the main post office so that you would get it early. For days afterwards, I had my share of the soul searching which every psychiatrist faces whenever a patient commits suicide.

I did not hear from you for a whole year. Then, caught in the glossy folds of a conference brochure, there was a postcard. You had needed to speak to me desperately. It was about Om. Both of you went to the same college, I remembered. The postcard said that he had become 'very strange' and was hearing 'horrible murmurings like mother used to.' I sensed your panic.

You had given a neighbour's phone number. When I rang up, the woman on the other end was suspicious, even after I told her I was from the hospital. It was only after I made it clear that I was calling about Om that she agreed to summon you to the phone. I could hear her shuffling step through the wire, and her muttered disparagement, that the boy belonged in the pagal-khana. When you finally came on the line, I urged you to bring Om to the clinic without delay, since if even the neighbours were noticing changes, it seemed serious.

It took three days for you to come, followed by a shambling, muttering Om, a far cry from the shy, finicky boy who had looked after his mother so lovingly. When I caught a glimpse of him in the waiting room, Om was in much worse shape than the postcard had revealed. He had not eaten for three days and had barely slept. The kurta-pyjama he wore and had refused to change was splattered with dried mud. He had a week-old stubble, and muttered ceaselessly with an animated expression. When he saw me, he tried to run away, and both the hospital orderlies had to restrain him. Then he cried and pleaded to be saved from the bearded men with green armbands and their sickles. I wondered how you'd managed to bring him all the way to Chandigarh on your own in this state.

By the time his turn came in the OPD, Om had begun to curse, ceaselessly and repetitively. He plugged his ears with his fingers, and seemed baffled that this did not muffle the obscenities. Your eyes had welled up, but you turned your face away. When you turned back to speak to me, you looked resolute once again.

Om had always been the shy and distant one among you three siblings. Since your mother's death, he had withdrawn even more. He had no friends, but that had never seemed to bother him. When not studying, he was content to listen to cricket commentary on the radio or collect old European stamps, of which he had an impressive collection. You were a popular girl, but even your friends found it awkward to relate to him. He had also acquired a habit of smirking when sitting alone. When asked, he would vaguely reply, 'Oh, nothing,' or 'It was something I heard on the radio.' Lately, he would snap, 'Have personal jokes been banned in this country now?'

He had also taken to writing a diary of sorts and would remain awake diligently filling page after page. You had chanced upon it while tidying up his bed and were shocked to see that it was two hundred pages full of words like 'energy', 'god', 'sun', 'moon' and 'Om', interconnected in all possible permutations with arrows and stars and symbols that you did not understand. There were words like 'soulwolfer' and 'existencepump' that you'd never heard of.

Om told us later, when he was in a position to communicate, about what was happening to him. For six months, he had been having an uncanny feeling, as if things were in reality not what they seemed to be. He was living in a world where random events were intimately related to him in one way or another. Everything happening around him had an 'as if' quality. Shopkeepers and cart vendors on the street behaved as if they were actors hired to keep an eye on him. The barber wished him heartily as if he was expecting him. The pointed scissors kept moving too near his jugular as if they had a life of their own. One day, as he entered the bus, somebody at the front laughed and Om's hair stood on end. The stone lions at the fountain square were snarling at him, while spewing water from their mouths. Perplexed as he was by the hostility coming his way from everyone and everything, he could not put his finger on anything specific. It was as if the whole universe was waiting for a signal to pounce upon him. But when he thought about it logically, his alternate reality passed through his fingers like quicksand, and he had nothing to show to you or anybody else.

Then, one morning, while walking on the street, Om had his moment of epiphany. The strange happenings of the last six months abruptly fell into place like the pieces of a jigsaw. There were real people trying to murder him. It was a conspiracy that had been planned for months. The stone lions were animated remotely. They had killed the real barber and planted a fake one. The men in the bus were put there by the ISI to read his thoughts.

That was when he started hearing the voices which jeered at his manliness and told him conversationally that a tiny device had been planted in his head and his brain was now being controlled by a man named Jeevanditta, who had been dead for two hundred years, but worked through a proxy in Pakistan.

You were alarmed by the complexity of Om's symptoms and had asked me if it was a different illness than your mother's. I had tried to explain while the underlying issue was the same, the symptoms were probably so much more elaborate because Om was more educated. 'Your mother would not have implicated the ISI because she would not have been aware of its existence. His fear of Muslims with sickles is probably something borrowed from your mother's account though.'

Om remained in the hospital for a month and, like his mother, recovered very well. The voices disappeared. His fears were gone. Jeevanditta was a product of his stupid imagination. He would play table tennis with me in the ward and even win.

When you came to collect him, I explained that continuous medication on a 'long-term indefinite basis' was crucial for his complete recovery, and to prevent relapses. The words seemed to darken your face, or so I thought in the failing light of that rainy afternoon. When I turned back after switching on a light, you were gone.

~

A year passed and there was no postcard from you. No news was good news, I thought. Then, there it came, a pale corner peeping out from under a heap of mail. You now wanted to bring in Chitra, who seemed to be behaving oddly, over and above her regular fiery temper. She believed that a 'mussalman' doctor had killed your mother, despite all assurances to the contrary. I was aware that mental illness often ran in families and bred true to type. I also knew you three lived with your lives intertwined physically and emotionally. There was a need to believe in the 'reality' of the others, howsoever bizarre it might appear to an outsider. The French called it *folie à deux* or *folie à famille* when it extended to a whole family, although the former is the generic term used for all shared psychoses. The delusion of Muslim men baying for blood and honour had been passed down through the family like a cursed heirloom. I looked at you, as you gave the details in your precise clipped manner. You had lost some of your self-assured look and it pained me. It should not have; I was a doctor. But, I couldn't stop thinking about the lines that became prominent on your forehead as you spoke; ones I did not remember seeing before. But you still looked me straight in the eye and sat erect in the chair without any hint of self-pity.

~

I had my own clinic now. For the last three years, you had been coming regularly once every month with Om or Chitra. You were a teacher in a government school by then. Om had tried his hand at teaching, but he did not last for more than a few weeks at any job. Students found him staid and bland. The boys would heckle, and a hurt Om would leave the job. Chitra kept sitting in front of the TV for hours and had put on several kilos. Your salary was just enough to run the house.

When you could not come, you sent postcards to convey the minutiae of your siblings' behaviour. The words were getting smaller because there was more to write, since now there were two persons to write about. I could barely read but sensed your dismay. I did try to reply to each one, but I was travelling a lot for conferences. Sometimes when I returned, I would find you sitting in the waiting room and your postcard in the mail. I would catch myself looking at the deepening lines on your dusky face as you explained Om and Chitra's progress or the lack of it.

I could also see that your savings were eroding fast and it was getting difficult to keep the stream of medication flowing. In the past, I had tried to pass on to you some of the 'Physician's samples' that drug reps leave with doctors, but you had refused, saying, 'These are for poor patients, the real poor ones. I do not think we are there yet.' One day, I managed to push some of those on to you. It seemed to me that when you went out your walk had lost some of the spring that always allowed me to recognize you from a distance. I wasn't sure if I was imagining it. I was not even sure if I had done the right thing.

A week later, on a blazing afternoon, I was in my office, writing the abstract of a paper for the next conference. The drone of the air-conditioner made me sleepy and I was thinking of asking for a cup of coffee. Just then, the door burst open. I saw you with your hair open and dupatta trailing, sobbing loudly. My first thought was that Om had killed himself. It was much worse.

'Dr Kohli,' you shouted at me between loud wails, 'Om and Chitra are not mentally ill, nor was my mother. There are real bearded mussalman men out there, hundreds of them, carrying swords, shouting that they will kill us. I heard them! They can become small like Lilliputians, and crawl through the ventilators. I saw them!

'You bastard! You have been pumping drugs into my brother and sister. You are on their side. You killed my mother too. You are a psycho yourself, a killer.' As you sprang forward to claw my face I looked into your dark tormented eyes full of tears and my heart sank. The nurses, who had heard the commotion, came in and prised you away. You continued screaming curses at me as they escorted you out.

You fell silent and turned at the door, gathering yourself up for a moment into a semblance of the determined, quiet woman who had sat opposite me so many times. You said softly, 'You loved me and wanted everyone out of the way. You should have told me, Prakash.'

For a long time, I sat dazed. Then I simply put my head down on the table and cried.

The last time I had cried was when my father had gone out and got himself killed by a stray bullet. It was a similar blazing afternoon.

THE MAD PROPHESIER

The Impala is still stuck in Gawal Mandi, surrounded by auto rickshaws packed with boisterous boys in cricket jerseys, and carrying bats, pads and gloves, probably going home after a practice game. The laden pick-up vans parked in front of the shops narrowed the road. Burkha-clad shoppers with their face veils upturned were walking briskly through the gaps in traffic. It is the last day of Prakash's visit.

Salman and Shaukat are trading Maulana Maududi jokes. It is Salman's turn, 'According to the Mullah-in-Chief, if a man utters "talaaq" three times, even before marriage, the woman he weds will be instantly divorced!'

Mehmood turns back and tells Prakash, 'Do not listen to him. He is mad. He's on medication.' To prove his point, he stretches his hand around the seat and takes out two strips of capsules from its flap. Salman snatches at them, but then gives them to Prakash.

'Yes, so what if I am on medication? I could not sleep and had this crazy weepiness. I would howl every morning like a slapped child. My mother said I just did it to get out

of going to college, because where does the crying go in
the evenings? I would happily see TV with everybody at
night. I pointed out that I cried on Sunday mornings too...

'Shaukat took me to this doctor here in Lahore. He
said I have depression and depression is always worse in
the mornings. I don't howl now, but I have to take this
medicine for six months.'

Prakash's mind latches itself on to the possibility that
he could meet a Pakistani psychiatrist. He asks Shaukat,
who nods without turning and swerves to enter a side lane
joining a wider road. Twenty minutes of crawling behind
tongas and autorickshaws later, he takes a U-turn to drive
along a quaint canal bordered by trees. Strapping lads, the
younger ones with nothing on, jump off the dark wooden
bridges that straddle it, and splash noisily, heedless of the
evening chill.

All of a sudden, they are in a classy neighbourhood
with tree-lined roads, neat lawns, manicured hedges and
armed guards at tall gates. The car stops at the only gate
which is wide open. A smiling Pashtun boy hobbling on
a crutch allows them in without a question. The over-
sized name plate says 'Dr Asif Junaid Hussain, Consultant
Psychiatrist. 6–8 p.m. Friday Closed.'

Apparently Dr Hussain has a day job elsewhere. He
seems to be using his study as the evening clinic, and the
lawn, now full of people, as a waiting area. Most people are
standing since there are only two benches. Shaukat makes
the unusual request that a visiting Indian psychiatrist
wishes to meet Dr Hussain.

A short thin man in an unwashed shalwar-kameez, sitting sandwiched between two women on a bench, shouts at the younger one, 'You slut around with the butcher's son, and I am mad because I cannot bear to see this happening before my eyes? You said you wanted my cough fixed and bring me here to a brain doctor!' He was both angry and pleading, now addressing the older woman, apparently his mother, 'What is this insaaf?'

Shaukat calls for Prakash. The boy with the crutch calls another name. There is a minor commotion and Prakash finds himself in the doctor's chamber, along with the emaciated man with a delusion and his two women escorts. The older woman walks with the help of a polished bamboo stick, tapping it loudly before her as if testing the ground, before taking the next step.

A tall, handsome man in a dark Savile Row suit and ruffled hair, grown long, apparently out of neglect than style, comes around the table and hugs him closely, heart to heart, as if they were close relatives meeting after years, not utter strangers. He complains in Punjabi, 'You should have written. I would have organized something. More of us could have met you.' Then, in a practical tone, 'When do you leave?'

'I have been told that if I do not leave tomorrow, I will be put in Kot Lakhpat jail.'

Asif shakes his head unhappily, waves a hand around the room as if apologizing for the fact that he has to see patients and returns to his revolving chair. Prakash finds himself seated in the only other chair at the edge of the table. The skinny man sits on a bench against the wall, hemmed in by his veiled wife and his plump mother, who taps the floor with her stick to remind the doctor that they were there first.

'Oh, I do apologize,' Dr Hussain says charmingly as he faces the trio. 'Tell me Bilal,' he asks, reading the name from a slip of paper on his table, 'What is wrong?'

Over the next one and a half hours, Prakash observes as Asif handles his patients delicately. Asif studiously avoids introducing him to patients. 'That would have been too much for them to process,' he explains later. Prakash understands, of course, and is content to be an observer.

The window panes were dark now. Sometime during the evening, coffee and biscuits had been served. Asif said, 'Just one last patient.'

This time, Prakash was introduced immediately as a 'dear colleague from the other side'. This last person seemed to be an exception in other ways as well. 'Mr Haq is a client.' Prakash noticed the substitution of the word 'patient'. Asif continued, 'He needs me off and on for what he calls his "blue funks".'

Mr Haq looked like a mid-level executive on his way back from work. The loose tie, wrongly buttoned jacket, grey hair showing through indifferently applied henna and grim moustache-less upper lip corroborated 'blue funks' alright. He nodded at Prakash, who thought he'd seen a momentary glimmer in the dull eyes at the mention of Prakash being from India.

He came straight to the point. 'No I am not better, Dr Hussain. Worse, in fact. The whole day is a drag. It is now like a dark shadow drawn over the whole day, not just the evenings like before. Why don't I resign? It is not fair to the company. It's not even a proper medical reason for not working well. That's why I do not ask for these expenses to be reimbursed.'

'You should not resign, because soon you will be out of it and then you will regret resigning. And then we would be grappling with an entirely different blue funk,' Asif explained.

'How can I come out of it when he is in the hospital battling hundreds of poking tests and hurtful procedures? Our newspapers give just a few lines, and Indian papers are not available here.' Mr Haq turned to Prakash, 'You would know. How are his test reports?'

Prakash was thoroughly nonplussed.

'Mr Haq is talking about Amitabh Bachchan. He is in hospital, apparently with a suspected diagnosis of myasthenia gravis. The last time Mr Haq needed me was a year and a half ago, when Amitabh Bachchan was in a coma, after a fight scene went wrong during shooting. That was the longest blue funk Mr Haq has had. Six months. He and Mrs Haq flew to Mecca to pray for Amitabh Bachchan to get well, so that Mr Haq, too, could get well. He didn't work for those six months. The company almost fired him, since he had not told them anything. He feared that he would be ridiculed. And it so happened that soon after Mecca, the actor quickly recovered and Mr Haq rejoined his work.'

'Whenever I slept then, I dreamt of dead bodies in red uniforms. Those dreams are back. Dead bodies in red uniforms with brass badges lying on railway platforms. My wife insists that it is a sign we should go to Mecca again.'

'But that was not the first time, Mr Haq?' Asif asked for Prakash's benefit.

'No, the first time was many years back. It was just a viral fever he had. I was fine in two weeks. A short blue funk. We were thirty-four then.'

'These two gentlemen were born on the same day, at the same time, in the same city,' Asif informed Prakash. 'The senior Mr Haq taught English at Allahabad University.'

Mr Haq was crying now without any pretence. Tears flowed down the sides of his clean-shaven upper lip into the hennaed beard as he asked, between sobs, 'Is it true that people die of myasthenia because they cannot breathe?'

Asif told him about the medications for myasthenia and that it was treatable in most cases.

'I also worry about his future. Our future. He is getting old and will keep having one or the other health issue as a matter of course. Then what will happen to me? And I have my own illnesses, you know, high blood pressure and diabetes. Barely controlled. Why don't I just die?'

Asif gently pushed the box of tissues lying on his table towards Mr Haq.

'Scores of children must have been born in the same city that night. I am sure they do not share his illnesses as you do. What makes you think that you two are joined at the hip? He does not even know you exist.'

'I agree. Madness, it is Dr Hussain, and that is why I am here.'

There was a weak attempt at a smile. Mr Haq listlessly pushed the fresh prescription into his pocket, waved at Prakash feebly and walked to the door. He turned just before going out, 'I think I will miss the appointment next week. Might as well listen to the missus and go to Mecca.'

'And whose health will you and Mrs Haq pray for? Yours or his?' Asif asked.

'His, of course, Dr Hussain. I will recover automatically, inshallah.'

The lights in the lawn had been switched on. It was past nine in Pakistan, nine-thirty in India. Jasmeet would have switched off the TV. Prakash felt chilly in his cotton shirt and wondered for the first time about what his three escorts had done all evening.

'They have gone to fetch your bag. You are sleeping here tonight.' Asif spoke casually, with his head bent while he locked the table drawer, as if inviting somebody he had just met to sleep in his house was the most natural thing in the world. 'My wife and daughter are away in Karachi. We will talk.'

Prakash did not feel awkward that he hadn't been formally invited. He thought of the conventional phrases, 'not wanting to be a cause of inconvenience', 'not wanting to impose', but did not actually utter anything. Instead, he said, 'I wanted to visit the mental hospital tomorrow morning before I leave. Can you please organize it?'

'Organize it? I will take you there... No! Tomorrow is my OPD day. But I can take you there right now. Remember, the best time to visit a hospital is at night. Pluses and minuses show up clearly.'

A car stopped outside. It was the Impala. His bag was deposited with the Pashtun boy who slung it around his shoulder and carried it into the house, without the crutch, hopping all the way. A flurry of addresses and telephone numbers being exchanged and of promises to meet again was followed by several rounds of hugs and pumping of hands. Salman clung to Prakash and sobbed. Finally, the Impala glided away, with Prakash absent-mindedly touching his navel and looking as if he too was about to cry.

Asif had meanwhile reversed his car into the street—a brand new hatchback with the logo 'Pakistan Suzuki Co.' on the bonnet. The plastic still covered the rear seat and there was the familiar new-car smell.

The canal flowed quiet and dark at that hour. It was a short drive, and Prakash felt his anticipation growing as the hospital came into sight. They stopped at an imposing gate like that of a fortress. The two engraved columns were topped with short minarets. A tall old man in a baggy Pathan suit flung the gate open with a couple of slick movements. They got down and Asif made the introductions, 'Khan Sahib has been manning this gate at night, since before Partition.' Dilshad Khan said 'Khushaamdeed' several times and asked Prakash about Amritsar where he had spent his childhood with his father, an itinerant pistachio vendor, hawking their goods in the narrow lanes around the Golden Temple.

Well-kept flower beds flanked the roads inside the campus, with the lawns beyond the flowers wrapped in an inky darkness. The car glided gently over speed breakers, implying an easy familiarity between the driver and the road. Asif stopped in front of an old but well-preserved office block, the same that his father had once occupied. They walked through a dark corridor lined with potted plants. A door was ajar with the lights on inside. The green name-plate read, in white letters:

Dr Salma Ansari, MBBS
Deputy Medical Superintendent

Asif stood dramatically outlined in the door frame, while Prakash was still several steps behind, hidden in the darkness of the corridor. 'Wow, finally, a woman as the night deputy. A first for Mental Hospital, Lahore. Should have been a headline in the morning paper!'

'My my, if it isn't the hot-shot psychiatrist Asif Junaid Hussain himself! Let me guess. You finally lost your marbles and have come to be secretively loony binned, so that you don't lose your flourishing practice. And since you're a clever lunatic, you chose the night when your first cousin—and fourth love interest—is on duty.'

Since a private conversation seemed to be going on, Prakash had continued to linger in the corridor. Now, as Asif turned towards him, he came up, feeling a little awkward. It was a small room. There was an old office table with a chipped wooden surface and a shaded lamp hanging from the ceiling. Steel shelves filled with files and registers lined its walls. A window looked upon the driveway, revealing Asif's Suzuki, parked in a hurry, with the driver's door wide open. A flashlight stood on the wide window sill while a copy of Eugene Blueler's *Textbook of Psychiatry* lay open on the table and a small pack of Marlboro Lights completed the picture.

Tall and fair, Salma was an exceptionally good-looking young woman. 'But you have company and I am terribly embarrassed. You should have warned me,' she said as she rose from the table, trying to rearrange the dupatta of her black salwar-kameez.

'That is okay. Those were no state secrets that you spilled.'

Before Asif could introduce them, Salma asked Prakash, 'You are an Indian, no?'

'Does it show?'

'It shows from a mile away. This thing about Indians and Pakistanis being so much like each other, like identical twins separated at birth, has been done to death, I think. It is just another sentimental Punjabi orgy.'

'You exaggerate the difference, but I'm impressed by your spot diagnosis,' Prakash took the chair offered by Salma.

'In any touristy city abroad, I can tell the two apart through the wrong end of a telescope—and I don't just mean Sardarjis. In Pakistan of course, you guys stand out like sore thumbs, as we would in India, I'm sure.'

Asif made another attempt at introductions, 'Prakash is a psychiatrist from Chandigarh. Salma Ansari, psychiatrist-in-making, feminist, political analyst, India baiter, writes for the *Dawn* regularly and, as you heard, is my first cousin. Our parents—well, her parents and my mother—wanted us to marry, but Salma wisely chose an Army officer. He's a frequent flier to Mecca, and thanks to religious merit, will be a full General one day.'

'Now, those *are* state secrets being spilled and jealously does not suit you, cousin Asif,' Salma carried the banter on but was clearly uncomfortable with Asif's outspokenness.

'So, Pakistanis are very different from Indians is what you believe?' Prakash prompted.

'Yes, we are taller, fairer—would be much higher on the Caucasian index if there was one. We are the ones who came from Central Asia and Persia. You guys were born here. We speak better Punjabi, write better English—go and compare the features in the *Dawn* and the *Times of India* on any given day. We wear better-designed clothes, drive more stylish cars.' She looked at the hatchback parked outside the window and carried on, 'Asif is an exception. He is quite an Indian actually. You are welcome to take him and the car back with you. Nobody, least of all Mirrat, who I can bet a thousand bucks is in Karachi today, will miss him,' she finished, looking again at the open car door.

'Wow! You forgot cricket. You play better cricket. Yes?'

'Yes, of course, except that I love Sunil Gavaskar!'

'But he is an Indian.'

'I concede that, with some effort, it is possible to love even an Indian.' The bright coquettish smile negated the sarcasm every time.

Prakash liked sparring with this razor-sharp woman. 'You are an India-baiter. You should be nastier. You should say that being bigger, India can provide a level of comfort to Pakistan, so that you spend less on bombs and more on welfare and that India deliberately does not do it, because it wants Pakistan to keep buying arms till it goes broke.'

'But it's absolutely true. You do want us to go broke and go begging, so that you can say, "Have you had enough of your Pakistan? We told you the whole idea was batty to begin with!"' she said charmingly.

They had a late dinner of tea and samosas from the canteen and mutton biryani from Salma's tiffin box. An Urdu newspaper, with an outsized picture of President Zia-ul-Haq delivering a talk at a military school graduation parade was their makeshift tablecloth. The tea was thick, strong and sweet, like the tea in canteens all over the subcontinent, but the samosas had a distinct cinnamon flavour.

Prakash looked at the registers lining the steel cupboards along the walls and asked Salma, 'You've heard of the transfer of Hindu and Sikh patients from this hospital to India, and reciprocally, of Muslim patients in Indian hospitals to here?'

'Yes, of course. Everybody knows about that.'

'Do you know that about three hundred patients died in this hospital in three years while waiting for their transfer? That is, about half the patients that should have been transferred?'

'How can so many people die?' Salma asked with a journalist's curiosity.

Prakash looked down at his feet to avoid looking at her, expecting ridicule. 'Some would have died a natural death in three years. Others…were killed.'

'Psychiatry does get to some of us, howsoever we may deny it to laymen,' Salma said with some irritation.

Prakash ignored the jibe, 'My guess is that if you looked at the annual reports of those three years, you would find sky-high death rates, all from natural causes of course. But if you looked closely, you would find that death was partial towards a particular religion. I can also bet a decent amount of money that the ghastly death rates came back to normal suddenly in 1951. So that is the homework for you, if you are really interested. Prove that Pakistani journalists are better than Indian amateurs like me.'

'Wait, wait. You said, "killed". How and why were they killed?'

'There are many ways of killing a mental patient, without even lifting a finger. He gets dysentery; nobody does anything about it. He dies. Simple.'

'Who gained by their deaths? Where is the logic?' Salma desperately needed this stranger to be wrong.

Asif, who'd been sitting and smoking Salma's Marlboros, spoke for the first time, 'Who gained by the deaths of one million people? Where was the logic? The partition of mental hospitals was an extension of the Partition of India. So people died here too. Only difference was the modus operandi and the cold-bloodedness.'

'Happened in India too, if it makes you feel any better,' offered Prakash. Seeing Salma's troubled expression. 'I have talked to people who know it happened and in an identical fashion.'

Dimmed headlights lit the window-pane for a fraction of a second, and they heard just a touch of the horn. It was one in the morning, time for the night deputy's rounds. Salma asked them to join her. The twelve wards, Prakash was told, were spread across eighty acres and the night doctor took the rounds in a jeep. They all trooped outside.

A youngster in an army uniform gave a sharp salute to Salma. He drove a jonga painted in green and yellow camouflage patterns, like a combat vehicle. As they drove, Prakash saw that the flowerbeds were lined with bricks, painted white. The long rows shone in the dark. The hedges were trimmed. The whole campus wore the look of an army cantonment.

'Our director is an army brigadier,' Salma seemed to be reading his mind. 'Serving, not retired. He is not a psychiatrist. The last person you need to administer a hospital as big as this is a psychiatrist. No offence to present company.' Prakash was not sure if she was being sarcastic.

They drove to the wards, one by one. Each ward was a high-roofed, massive brick structure with a front porch in the centre, the only part lit up at that hour. Each waiting night nurse stepped out of the porch and reported while standing in the headlights of the jeep. 'Everything is fine. All patients are calm. There is nothing special to report.' Men manned the male wards and women the female. There were no exceptions to the routine.

The twelfth ward was in the backyard of the hospital, used only to seclude patients who were very disruptive on a continuous basis. The road to it petered out soon, and the jeep passed below the low branches of a banyan tree which covered the front of the whole ward. There was no nurse waiting here. A greenish mould had turned the steps slippery. The only illumination was from the headlights of the jeep. A jerky point of light at a distance turned out to be an approaching torch. A tall man emerged from the building and informed Salma, 'It's the transformer, I'm afraid. It will have to wait till the morning.'

There were just three patients in Ward 12 that night, each isolated in a cell of his own. There were no patients in the main ward, Prakash was told. The cells were a row of holes in the corridor walls, shut by heavy doors with rusting bars and over-sized latches. The empty cells were also locked from the outside. Most cells functioned as stores for supplies. There were boxes of all shapes and sizes, with Urdu labels. In the fleeting light, Prakash thought he read Hoor Beauty Soap, Umar Sarwar motorbike shoes and Naqshbandi hair dye. The labels perplexed him, but he could not be sure since the light was bad and his Urdu as rusty as the clunky bolts. Some cells stored medicines which carried labels in English.

They reached two occupied cells, facing each other. By the torchlight, he could see the huddled figures, one in each cell, wrapped in blankets and sleeping comfortably. 'Both were given injections at ten. They were hurling curses across the corridor. Had they not been locked in, they would have torn each other apart,' the nurse informed them.

Prakash looked at their peaceful faces, one with the fuzz of a new beard, the other probably too young for even that. Salma remarked, 'Brothers. Schizophrenia. Father gone to jihad, missing in action. Mother remarried. Cannot stand each other and try to gouge out each other's eyes. Problem is, if we separate them so that they can't see each other, they bang their heads against the walls and try to gouge out their own eyes. ECTs, depots, nothing has worked on them. A psychologist trained in Britain tried cognitive behaviour therapy. She tried to talk to them across the table. She is recovering from a torsion fracture in her arm.'

The ward proper was as big as a concert hall. It had cobwebs all over, and was a veritable graveyard of broken beds and torn mattresses lying atop each other. Jute and pieces of sponge spilled out, littering the floor. Prakash wondered about the hundreds of stories buried in those mattresses and twined around the bedposts. Salma looked up at the ceiling and asked, 'Where are the bats?'

'The brothers scared them away.'

She smiled for the first time during the rounds.

On the far side of the ward there were two more cells. The first was filled with tins labelled 'Kohinoor Basmati Rice—Approved by Rice Institute, Kala Shah Kaku'. Rats scurried about when the light moved along the floor.

Prakash had to ask, 'You must be the richest public mental hospital in the world to be able to feed basmati rice to patients. And give them hair dyes and beauty soaps and motorcycle shoes. I didn't see any motorcycles anywhere, though.'

'Be very careful. There is a steep step here. Doctors should focus on patients,' Salma replied cryptically.

They were at their last patient of the night. A man who could have been of any age between sixty and eighty sat calmly in the dark, a blanket neatly folded around his shoulders like a shawl, as if waiting for guests in his own drawing room. He had short hair and a pointed beard, both greying and giving him a distinguished air. The face was of the complexion known as wheatish, pock-marked and deeply furrowed. When the torchlight fell on his face, he squeezed his eyes shut and let out what sounded like a curse. The words he actually said were 'Oh, tera bhala hove,' but the benediction erupted like an expletive.

Prakash asked, 'Why is he in there? He looks composed enough.'

'Violent he has never been. He can be pretty coarse when angry. God knows where he learns so many brand-new abuses from. If he is let out, he starts digging right away. The sight of earth fires him up and he starts digging furiously like he is possessed. He uses whatever he can lay his hands on. A spade, a shovel, a sickle, a chisel, whatever. Once he stole a pair of scissors from the barber's room, another time, a knife from the kitchen. If nothing else, he saves the iron files the nurses use to snip injection ampoules.'

Prakash looked at the old man in the cell. He seemed to know what was being talked about, but appeared indifferent, even insolent. 'The maximum he has dug is two feet after a night of heavy rain,' continued Salma.

'But why is he here? Why not in one of the seclusion cells in the front wards? He is not noisy like the brothers.'

'Oh, staying here is his choice. He has spent forty years in this ward. He says there are memories here and he does not want to relocate at his age.'

'But he wants to escape from here at this age!'

'He has nowhere to escape to, no-one either. He digs in order to make a tunnel to connect this hospital to Amritsar Mental Hospital in India, forty-five kilometres away, to meet his friend Rulda Singh, who had been here with him at the time of Partition.'

Images of an afternoon during his internship many years ago throng Prakash's mind: a freak hailstorm, a plateful of hot samosas and a mild-mannered Sikh with swollen gums, talking about the 'Mental Hospital Express' which had carried Hindu and Sikh patients from Pakistan to India, and brought back Muslim patients on its return journey.

'Are you Fattu?' Prakash asked the man sitting cross-legged in the dark.

The torchlight scanned Fattu's face. He nodded, 'How is Rulda?'

Both Salma and Asif looked up at Prakash, clearly surprised.

'I met Rulda Singh in Amritsar,' Prakash explained to his hosts. 'But how would he know that?'

Fattu was enigmatic, 'I have a hot-line with Rulda,' he said, tapping his head. 'From here. You will not understand. Let's just say I made a wild guess. You are being taken around, so a visitor from outside, possibly a psychiatrist. Nobody else would go around talking to patients at midnight. And only Rulda could have told you my name.'

'To tell you the truth, I met him just once, a long time ago. He talked about you a lot. He missed you. He was fine then, but, well, after that I did not look him up.'

Fattu reassured Prakash. 'He is fine now too, had a talk with him just this afternoon, actually, about an Indo-Pak Mental Patients Forum that we are trying to put together. In order to exchange songs, to borrow ideas on how to escape ECTs, to share biryani and butter chicken, how to hit a sadistic warden without being caught, to share anti-lice powder when it is short, and so on and so forth. Matters of mutual interest, you know. But for all this we need a tunnel. We are collaborating on that project. Rulda told me the tunnel from his side has reached Wagah border and the rest is up to me. He said he cannot dig further because he does not have a visa.'

Salma burst out laughing. 'Fattu, you have such heart-to-hearts every day, what do you need a tunnel for?'

'I want to touch him like this.' He brought the tips of his index fingers together, in front of his chest. 'Besides, Salma Bibi,' he continued with an impish smile, 'with me being so mental, how do I know that the conversation is real or whether it is my confounded cranium echoing again?'

From under the tattered mattress that Fattu was sitting on, he produced a blank paper, folded it into four and passed it on to Prakash, 'Please give this letter to Rulda. Tell him that I had received his letter thirty-three years ago but being busy with this and that could not reply earlier. Tell Rulda Singh of Rawalpindi, currently resident of Mental Hospital Amritsar, that you met Fateh Mohammed of Hoshiarpur, currently resident of Mental Hospital Lahore.' With that, a tired Fattu lay down on his side, an arm under his head, facing the bars but apparently dismissing his audience.

The four of them continued past the ward. Prakash unfolded the paper. It was a blank sheet. There was a whitewashed wall at the far end of the corridor. With a piece of coal, somebody had written in an elegant handwriting, 'Jihad is ordained for you, though you dislike it. But it is possible that you dislike a thing which is good for you, and like a thing which is bad for you. But Allah knows, and you know not.' Precise chapter and verse were quoted.

Prakash asked Salma, 'Does he get any visitors?'

'He has no friends or relatives, but visitors he has—plenty. Lots of wannabe middle-level politicians and some people from the security agencies of the government.'

'Why the agencies?'

'Our Fattu here is famous. The agencies are interested in his digging activities. They are not even convinced that he is sick. Politicians come for his prophesies. He predicts events, big-ticket events. Like who will topple whom and when. Who will get the party seat and who will win. Stuff like that. He has never answered a straight question though. He just doles out gibberish when angry and throws around some weighty curses. He is supposed to have prophesied the breaking away of East Pakistan, two years before it happened....

'The reality was actually rather comic. Fattu had not taken a bath the whole winter of 1969. The other patients could not bear the stink and complained. A warden took off his clothes and forcibly bathed him. This was before he got into digging. Fattu got angry and let loose a litany of curses, intermingled with something about when the sun rises in the East, the Bengalis will keep their half and will send only half the sun to Punjab which will be wilted by the time it reaches. Take it any way, but when East Pakistan actually became Bangladesh after the War of 1971, the press went to town with the story from the warden who had hosed him down two years before. For all anyone knows, the warden may have made it up for his own two bits of glory. But it sure made Fattu famous.'

'And he also supposedly predicted Bhutto's hanging the day after he became prime minister,' Asif chimed in. 'The newspapers carried the photo of his swearing in. When somebody snatched Fattu's shovel—he was trying to prise away the veranda bricks—he gave one angry look at the paper and said, "Why is Zulfi walking as if he is being led to the gallows? Maybe he can see his future."'

'That was enough for the politicians to come asking him questions and pampering him with burfis—his favourite sweet. *I* think he is a trickster.'

As they passed Fattu's cell on their way back, Asif saw that he was awake. He bade him goodbye: 'Allah Hafiz, janaab Fateh Mohammad Sahib.'

There was an angry shout from the cell and all four turned around, surprised.

'Doctor Asif Junaid Hussain, I knew your father, may his soul rest in peace, and so can ask you with force, what happened to Khuda Hafiz?' Fattu seemed to be on fire. 'When did Allah Hafiz come and from where? I will tell you—when your children start counting backwards and mark my words, they will; they will know 1979 was the year when Khuda Hafiz became Allah Hafiz and Jannat Jannah. This is when the terra firma led into swamp and we happily walked deep into it, with our hands above our heads.' Fattu was incoherent with rage. His Punjabi now had a quaint hilly accent. Prakash remembered Rulda telling him that he came from a village on the foothills of the Shivalik mountains.

Between curses and stark anatomical descriptions, Fattu talked disjointedly about cities being named after erection-obsessed sheikhs, boys being slaughtered in the snow, girls being shot for singing mahiyas at weddings, airliners swallowing thousands of people in tall buildings for breakfast and a whole lot of cashews in school-children's satchels being drenched in blood. It was a prolonged jumble of words and sobs after that, and then he finally seemed to have exhausted himself. He lay down, spent and motionless, but just for a few moments.

Fattu spoke again, not in anger now, but with an unsettling composure. He said softly, in the dark, 'Tell Marde Momin not to go near Cholistan. The desert is tricky, like a woman. Sand is not good for man or machine. Or do me a favour. Do not tell him.'

'And you from the East,' Fattu was now looking piercingly at Prakash, 'Who told you that a Ghaznavi has to come only from Ghazni or even that it has to be a man? The woman Ghaznavi will die, but three mental hospitals full of Sikhs will also die. And much much later, half a score beasts will rise from the swamp and gobble up eight scores of people at dinner in the boom city on the other side of the ocean, when the moon will be a sliver, and the sea calm.'

They were all still. One could hear the even breathing of the two brothers. In sleep they breathed in perfect unison. Salma tried to joke, without conviction, 'Here is more prophesy material for us to fit into future events after they have happened.'

In the jeep, Prakash asked nobody in particular, 'What is the difference between Jannat and Jannah?'

Nobody answered.

~

Asif and Prakash walked to the car. Prakash looked at the wide open door on the driver's side and then at Asif, and thought about the way he'd not taken his eyes off Salma all evening. He asked, 'Do you actually have an OPD in the morning?'

Asif shook his head and switched on the ignition.

LOVE DURING ARMISTICE

Prakash awoke with a start. It was neither the rain hitting the asbestos sheets that made up the roof, nor the sharp crackle of firewood, that had disturbed his sleep. It was a more definite sound, like a scrape and rustle. Jasmeet, next to him, continued to sleep undisturbed. They were in a remote hilly cottage beyond Simla. Barefoot, he tiptoed over the wooden floor into the tiny sitting area, filled with a mellow glow from the embers in the fireplace. He picked up Jasmeet's shawl flung onto the back of a chair and wrapped it around his shoulders. He found his slippers and, bracing for a chilly draft, carefully opened the door a few inches. The black gleam of his motorbike visible by the dim light allowed by the awning reassured him. The two of them had driven up the hills from Chandigarh for a weekend getaway at Kufri, refusing to be browbeaten by the certain prospect of rain. The nurses' grapevine at the hospital had, of course, ratcheted up their relationship several notches.

What startled him was the sight of a young boy in school uniform lying face down on the seat, with his head on the handlebar, hands dangling by the sides and feet in drenched canvas shoes touching the muddy ground at awkward angles. Prakash, anxious and annoyed, patted the boy hard on his back. His white shirt was sopping wet. The kid squirmed and managed to straighten himself with difficulty. He looked perplexed and then surprised to find himself where he was. He wiped dribble with the back of his arm from a youthful round face with very short crew-cut hair, a style favoured by school headmasters in the hills.

'Who are you?' Prakash asked gently, trying not to sound offended.

'Brij Bhushan, 11B', the youngster in wet clothes said mechanically, gathering his school bag from the floor, where it had left a puddle.

'I mean what are you doing here?' Prakash said, tapping his wristwatch. It said 11.30 p.m. 'At this time? In this weather? Didn't you go home after school?'

No reply. Brij seemed not to have heard him. The rain was creating quite a racket now. He strapped the dripping school bag to his back and looked ready to walk back into the sheets of rain.

'Wait! Go after the rain stops. You can come in and wait.' Prakash, on an intuition, stopped himself just in time from adding, 'We can call your parents.'

Brij halted at the edge of the veranda uncertainly. Instinctively, Prakash stepped forward to steer him by the elbow through the door before he walked away. He gathered up the clothes strewn across a chair next to the fireplace, indicating Brij should sit there. Brij took off his wet school bag, placing it in a corner of the room on the floor. He prised open the tight wet knot of his school tie, pulled it open and laid it neatly on the top of the bag. Prakash asked him to take off the mud-spattered shoes and the wet socks too. The young man sat at the edge of an easy chair, gingerly at first, then rested his head on the back of the chair and within moments, comforted by the warmth from fireplace, was fast asleep. Prakash watched over the childlike face and on an impulse touched the forehead with the back of his hand. It felt hot in spite of being wet. He went to the bedroom and woke up Jasmeet, 'We have a young visitor and he has fever.'

Jasmeet, always the more pragmatic one, took charge. She opened the school bag and took out a damp exercise notebook which informed them that Brij Bhushan studied at DAV School, Simla. Suppressing a yawn, she dug into the bag again and came up with a school diary with a red plastic cover. It had his father's name, a home address in Lower Bazaar and a phone number. She picked up the receiver of the dial-less black phone lying on the mantelpiece above the fireplace and gave the number to the receptionist, who offered to shift the boy to the main hotel building, half a kilometre away, till the family came. She also offered to see if a doctor could be found at that hour. Jasmeet looked at the calm face of the boy asleep, thought about the fever and the rain, and said that it was not necessary and, looking sideways through a gap in her long hair, added that her husband was a doctor.

Telling Prakash to add some wood to the fire, she went

through the kitchen door to heat milk which she had saved for the morning tea, took out two tablets of Crocin from her purse and asked Prakash to wake up the kid. Brij got up, again looking confused about his surroundings, but dutifully took the medicine. His clothes had started to dry already. Prakash rinsed the glass in the kitchen and came back to take the third chair.

Jasmeet asked him, 'How did you reach here from Simla?' Having travelled the same way, a few hours earlier, she knew that it was twenty-five kilometres on a high mountainous road, with deep ravines on one side.

'I walked. I do it often,' Brij said airily, as if that part was the least important. Anticipating the question about weather, he said, 'I stopped on the way when the rain was heavy. I had left early.'

'After school?' Jasmeet enquired.

The boy nodded. 'My father beats me. He would have beaten me today also.'

'Why?' Jasmeet asked, trying to put on a brisk, professional tone.

'Because I write letters. I wrote one today too. The English teacher took it away and told my father on the phone.'

'What is wrong with writing letters? I write letters all the time. Is it a girl that you write to?' Jasmeet asked, trying to sound casual, as if she was talking about weather while pretending to be busy with the fireplace. Brij kept quiet. His hair having dried, his face was looking a bit more adult. He fidgeted under Prakash's gaze, fussing with the brass buckle of his belt which carried what looked like a school insignia, with two stiff flags in red and blue.

Jasmeet justified the protective tenderness that she was feeling for the boy with the unclouded face and delicate features, by telling herself that it was fine; she was not in the clinic. 'What is her name?' she asked, trying to comb her hair with fingers.

Brij looked at her, for the first time with a trusting expression. 'Benazir,' he said simply.

Jasmeet, with the air of someone who has finally discovered the key piece in a jigsaw, took the cup of black coffee that Prakash offered her and said, 'So she is a Muslim? And that is why your father does not want you to write to her? Is she in your school?' Brij shook his head slightly and Jasmeet presumed that it was in response to her last question.

The hotel and its cottages lay scattered on a hillock, a couple of hundred feet above the highway, and any vehicle which laboured up the steep road at that hour, particularly if one remembered the Indian car engines of the early seventies, was bound to be heard from far, now that the rain had stopped. Brij was suddenly alert and blurted accusingly, 'You called my father!'

Prakash tried to explain, 'You are running a fever. What were we supposed to do? You should be home in bed anyway.'

Sensing a trap, his eyes now deep with suspicion, Brij made a dart for his schoolbag and shoes. The tie and socks slid to the floor as he rushed to open the door. He turned back and asked Jasmeet politely, without any rancour, 'Was the milk poisoned?'

Jasmeet who had got up to plead with him not to go out, was taken aback. As she fumbled for a response, the door was flung open and a harried middle-aged man in a turtleneck sweater burst into the room and ran into Brij.

'Oh, I am so sorry,' he apologized profusely for having come in without knocking. The tired-looking visitor went back to the door to take off his wet chappals, glaring all the while at Brij whose gaze seemed to now be riveted to a spot on the floor.

'Please sit. He had fever but he is better now,' Prakash said.

While taking the chair vacated by his son, Sunil Kant Behal explained that he owned a small cafe in Lower Bazaar and lived above it with his wife and two sons. He concluded with another bout of apologies for having caused so much trouble through his good-for-nothing younger son. Prakash said reassuringly, 'Please do not apologize. There is no need.'

The embarrassed father replied, 'Of course there is. He ruined your night. You are obviously here on holiday, not to nurse truant boys who invite fever by walking for hours in the rain. It is not the first time I have had to apologize on his account. It has become a way of life for me. I am an expert at apologizing. Apologizing and collecting him from all sorts of places at odd hours is all that I have been doing these last two months,' he finished bitterly.

He looked self-consciously at the fingers of his right hand, smeared dark with grease, and explained, 'The carburettor got stuck. I forgot my handkerchief in a hurry.'

Jasmeet looked at the lines on the unshaven, hassled face and invited him to clean his hands at the washbasin in the kitchen. When he returned, he looked at Brij and asked acidly, 'Shall we go home? Unless Behal Sir has some more urgent business to attend to, around the hills. It is only one in the morning yet.'

Jasmeet had hesitated to intervene between father and son, but a look at the boy's stricken expression made her feel protective, 'He does not go home because you beat him up for writing letters to a girl. Apparently she is a Muslim. You should instead sit with him and talk.'

With Brij still standing in the corner biting a nail, Sunil turned in his chair to confront Jasmeet and said, 'Did he also tell you that he has written forty letters in two months?' Then, more in pain than anger, '"Apparently she is a Muslim" indeed! Is that what he told you? Do you know who the girl in question is? Benazir Bhutto, daughter of President Bhutto of Pakistan!'

For a moment, Jasmeet dismissed this as a private joke between father and son. Prakash, bringing coffee for Sunil, stumbled at the kitchen door, 'Has he seen her pictures in the newspapers?' This was long before television came to Simla.

'He has seen her once. On the Mall Road. It was two months back, when she was here with her father for the Simla Agreement.'

Prakash and Jasmeet had stopped at a restaurant in Simla on their way to Kufri. The walls were full of photographs and newspaper cuttings related to the recent India-Pakistan summit. There was even a photograph of the restaurant owner beaming proudly with some journalists from Pakistan who had visited his restaurant for coffee. In the wake of the fierce war which the two countries had fought six months earlier, a summit was an urgent necessity, particularly for Pakistan. It had not just lost the war, but half of the country. East Pakistan, separated from West Pakistan by two thousand kilometres of Indian landmass, had declared itself independent Bangladesh, after India had forced a surrender by the Pakistani army.

Sunil, leaning forward in his chair, looked at Brij and then at Jasmeet with eyes full of hurt and asked plaintively, 'When will the Partition of the two countries leave us alone? In front of my eyes, I lost my father to it when I was that old,' he said, nodding at Brij. 'And now my son.'

A piece of wet wood had begun smoking. Prakash added fresh wood, stoked the fire and opened the outer door just a bit. Jasmeet, trying to hold down her cough, asked 'What has Partition got to do with it? Aren't you stretching the point?'

Sunil said lamely, though with tears in his eyes, 'If there was no Partition there would have been no war and no Simla Agreement.' He added bitterly, 'She came to free her prisoners and condemned my son to the life of one.' Leaning against the wall, Brij gazed expressionlessly at the wooden beam in the ceiling. Prakash, now standing with his hands on the back of Jasmeet's chair, asked Sunil, 'What exactly happened?'

'You see, when the Pakistanis were here for four days, Simla was decked up like a bride. Everybody was excited. The summit was happening just six months after we won the war. Ninety thousand Pakistani prisoners of war were still in Indian custody, telling their families across the border, day in and day out on the radio, about how they were safe and well looked after by their Indian captors,' Sunil explained, trying to rub off another stubborn grease stain he had discovered on his wrist. 'The Indian government prolonged the charade deliberately. When the Pakistanis landed here for a compromise, we could afford to be magnanimous. Combine that with ever-gushing Punjabi sentimentality, and the social graces of the Pakistanis, and you had Simla fawning over the delegation, particularly the father and the daughter as if they were long-lost relatives. Shopkeepers called her their daughter and refused to accept money for her shopping.

'She chatted with some students of her age, standing on the Mall Road in front of a cafe, to make it look impromptu, although it was of course orchestrated. The whole road was cordoned off.' Sunil looked at Brij who was standing with his back against the wall staring vacantly at the fire. 'Our Brij here tried to pass through the cordon, and got pushed around because he insisted on joining the group. As an angry commando lifted his hand to hit him, Benazir, who had spotted the commotion, gestured to the soldier to let the boy go. Just then, the government minders decided that she had had enough interaction with Indian university students for the day and whisked her away.

'But what happened during those few seconds was enough for Mr Brij Bhushan Behal of DAV School, Lakkar Bazar, Simla to conclude that Kumari Benazir Bhutto, daughter of Shri Zulfikar Ali Bhutto, President of Pakistan, was head-over-heels in love with him. He is sure she had been for a while, even before leaving for India, even when she did not know that he existed...not that she knows that he exists now!' Brij's face had become smaller with every word spat out by his father. He now sat slumped on the wooden stool lying near the door, with his head against the wall, his hands in his lap.

Jasmeet who had been struggling not to seem judgemental, dropped all pretence. She looked at Sunil blurting angrily, 'You do not make it easy for him, do you? I think you are half the problem!'

'What have I done?' Sunil looked hurt.

On familiar territory now, Prakash gestured at the two of them to calm down. He looked at Brij, who had appeared to be briefly interested in proceedings when his father was being scolded, and asked sharply, 'How do you know this is how she feels?'

Far away, a clock struck two. It was probably the church. Prakash and Jasmeet had stopped in the afternoon to take pictures of the quaint cemetery where hundreds of British army men lay nestled against the pine-shaded mountain slope under crumbling gravestones behind a church. He wondered in passing why he had not heard the clock before; perhaps a change in direction of the wind or the rain having stopped or just a quirky clock, he mused.

Brij continued staring into the flames as if he had not heard the question.

Sunil answered Prakash, studiously avoiding looking at Jasmeet. 'She comes into his dreams and tells him secrets which even her father does not know. For instance, what she was going to wear the next morning, when she was in Simla.'

'Didn't I know beforehand that she was going to wear the silk sari with flowers at the function?' Brij asked his father angrily, suddenly feeling a need to defend himself, now that he was being ridiculed before strangers. 'She said she had not told her father yet, and she was telling me!'

'Well, if you knew, you kept it to yourself till even I knew from the pictures in the newspapers,' Sunil reminded him.

'I scratched it on a rock at the Jakhu hill. It is still there. Go and see. She even told me about the black shirt and cream bell-bottoms.' Brij's fever seemed to have gone. He was willing to argue point by point with his father, especially after noticing that the charming lady with the long hair was on his side.

'And you scratched that bit about bell-bottoms too, on a rock in the hills? Who knows when? I have no problem with whatever madness it is, as long as it stays in your dreams. My problem is the police and the snooping detectives who come every time you write a letter. All of

Lower Bazaar comes to know that there has been another letter. Shopkeepers taunt me by asking when they should expect to go to Pakistan with the baraat. Should they ask the tailors to start stitching new dresses…tailors take time, you see, one jeers. Another one laughs asking, "Is it true that the bride is older than the boy by two years?"

'Brij quarrelled a lot with his classmates throughout those days,' Sunil looked at Jasmeet and continued in a gentler tone, 'because the boys were unhappy with so much affection being ladled out to people from an enemy country. Boys are like that you know, and the war had been so recent. I say, we went overboard as hosts. The government barred the public from the Ritz theatre for three days. The Pakistani guests wanted to watch *Anarkali*, *Mughal-e-Azam*, *Chaudhvin ka Chand* and whatnot. Mall Road was barricaded because the Pakistanis were coming to shop and sample Guruprasad's paan. The schoolboys resented this and Brij was roughed up when he argued with them about the duties of a host. He had to be given stitches on his forehead. Another time, when he waxed eloquent about Benazir Bhutto's grace and dignity even with her country in such a humiliating position, the boys made fun of him. He came home and hit his brother over a trifle. Twice, the police brought him home because he was found loitering around the Governor's house. He told me later that "she" had called him there.'

The door blew open because of the wind and then banged itself shut. Prakash got up to bolt it. The electricity went off. Brij's face glowed in the light from the fireplace,

'Papa what should I do? It is true. It is true!' With that, he started crying helplessly.

There was the hum of a generator starting somewhere above them on the hill, and the tubelight flickered back to life. Sunil looked at his watch and got up with a start. He apologized all over again, thanked them both profusely with folded hands, took Brij by the hand and carrying the school bag and tie in his other hand, went out. Prakash and Jasmeet came to the door.

The rain had stopped but it was still very windy. Sunil's Fiat refused to start. He sheepishly waved, as if requesting them to return inside. He tried a few times more and then as if re-enacting a practised drill, Brij jumped out briskly, went to the rear, pushed the car, his head down and cheeks puffed out. When they reached a downward slope, he ran back to get in, as Sunil pulled back the handbrake. As the car glided down and the engine spluttered, Jasmeet pulled Prakash into the cottage, laughing, 'So much for our first night out together.'

* * *

A year passed, during which Prakash would remember the stormy night in the Simla hills and their besotted young visitor, whenever he saw a news report about Zulfikar Ali Bhutto.

Prakash was now the duty resident at the Post Graduate Medical Institute in Chandigarh. One night, when a student nurse dropped the case files of the day's new admissions on his table, he read the large bold letters, 'Brij Bhushan

Behal'. It was him all right, with the correct father's name and the Lower Bazaar, Simla address. The meticulous history written in the outpatient form mentioned the Simla Agreement as the 'precipitating factor'.

It went on to describe at length the 'patient's preoccupation with Benazir Bhutto to the exclusion of everything else' and 'a delusional belief that she visits him in dreams and the two have long conversations…. The patient firmly believes that Benazir Bhutto loves him, but because of her father being the Prime Minister of Pakistan and the two countries being bitter enemies, cannot admit it openly; hence the nocturnal visits. For some months, after the onset, the patient used to write frequent letters to her, care of Radcliffe College, Cambridge, MA, USA. Patient says that this address was given to him by her in one of the dreams. This happens to be the correct address, according to patient's father, who thinks that he may have read it in a magazine. The letters were intercepted by police who came to investigate each time.

'However, he stopped writing to her because now she "visits" him frequently and letters are "no longer needed". Patient is also aware that she has recently moved to Oxford University in the UK. He says this too was told to him by BB, the initials by which he refers to her fondly. He says that they happen to be his initials too, and she also calls him by the same name. He admits when asked that he does not have access to her dreams. When pressed for the reason, he says that the Department of Dreams is much stricter that side, but she is trying to procure the code for him.

'Always a sober, studious student who used to get excellent grades, patient failed his higher secondary examination and managed to just pass it the following year. Both he and his father were keen that he join college, but by then, everybody in the town knew about his "problem" and no college in Simla agreed to admit him.

'The patient was taken to a local psychiatrist who advised rest and medication. However, the father stopped the medicines, when one night Brij was found walking on the Sanjauli highway in a groggy condition. He barely escaped being run over, according to a tea-stall owner. Brij was taken to another psychiatrist who advised a different medication which worked and made the "dreams" much less, but which the patient refused to take for that very reason.

'Patient says that he and Benazir often have long political discussions which range from friendly banter to heated arguments. When asked for an example, he mentioned that she was miffed with him for insisting that Kashmir belonged to India. The patient had argued that although the majority of the population of Kashmir was Muslim, it had a Hindu king who signed the accession treaty with India. She, according to him, angrily countered that Junagarh had a Muslim king who had signed an accession treaty with Pakistan, but the state was still forcibly occupied by India, with the argument that the majority of Junagarh's population was Hindu. The patient thinks that she has a point because you cannot look at the religion of the king in one state and the religion of the population in another state for deciding which way the state should go.

'He also laments on her behalf that the ninety thousand prisoners which India had promised to release have still not been freed a year after the Simla Agreement. The patient angrily insists that this amounts to breach of trust.'

There was more about how the patient had recently started to stay out for days, after his mother casually mentioned that she would like to get the two sons married at the same time. He would roam the hills day and night, in rain and sleet, and would come back on his own in a dishevelled condition, often sick with cough and fever. The family, according to the out-patient resident, had started to show signs of 'carer fatigue' and had stopped looking for him when he went away.

Prakash looked for the bed number on the file. It was of one of the private rooms down the corridor. Patients in the rooms slept earlier than those in the ward, so he walked quietly to see if Brij was awake. The light was switched off, but the door was open a couple of inches. In the light from the corridor, he saw Sunil and Brij deep asleep in the same bed, with Brij's arm thrown carelessly around his father. Prakash smiled and thought that Benazir Bhutto still had some work to do. He was wrong.

The next day, Prakash left the hospital early. He had to catch a train to Delhi for a seminar. When he returned after three days, he was told by the wide-eyed breathless student nurse, that the boy from Simla who had 'delusions of erotomania' had absconded from the hospital. For three consecutive nights he had not had his dream, and he blamed the treatment.

~

Another two years went by without news of Brij. Prakash remembered the young boy from the hills with his unusual malady only when coming across news about Pakistan. Then, one early winter morning, as he was coming out of Delhi airport, tired and spent after a much-delayed flight from Europe, a man in a long coat and a Kullu cap stepped forward from the row of people waiting to receive their relatives and stood in front of him, looking as surprised as Prakash himself. It was Sunil Kant Behal. He had come to receive his elder son, who was returning from Switzerland after completing a course in hotel management. Prakash pulled his trolley out of the way to talk to him. He asked him about Brij and was told that he had not been seen after the night he ran away from the hospital, two years ago.

'Do you know anything about his whereabouts?' Prakash asked.

'Someone I know met him in Ajmer last week. Brij said he had been waiting for a special guest from Pakistan, somebody who had told him about coming to Ajmer Sharif, not through a letter or a telegram, but in a dream.' Sunil's attention was drawn by his elder son coming towards them from the airport entrance. As he waved, Prakash asked, 'Are you sure it was him? There are many people like that at dargahs. Did your friend know him?'

'No, my friend did not know him, but it was him all right. He had a tattoo on his arm which read "Brij Bhushan Bhutto",' Sunil tossed over his shoulder, as he went forward to receive his son.

REFUGEES

'Is it Partition time again?' Ma asked when I drove her to the station to put her on a train.

Feeling her heart pounding against my chest, I patted her on the back and said, 'Don't be silly. Partitions do not happen every day.'

But that was later.

~

Motorists on the Chandigarh–Zirakpur road could not see the sign unless they were looking for it. Jasmeet, who is an Urdu aficionado, had given the names Armaan to the house and Ahsaas to the hospital.

'Armaan is desire, and Ahsaas, understanding,' she had translated for Anhad several years later. And she was the one who insisted that the sign for the house should be discreet. 'It is our home, not an airport, please,' she had argued with the painter, who was peddling a bigger board.

The shrubbery, overgrown after the rains, had covered most of the sign. The gravel path, now mossy, was shadowed by a long canopy of trees. Twigs remained stuck under the wipers of our cars. The path ended at a wrought-iron gate

which led to a driveway, dark even during the day because
the trees were even denser here. When the house was built,
the gate was unmanned and the boundary wall shoulder-
high. The wall went up a couple of feet every time there was
a shooting or a rich man's son got kidnapped. 'History in
these parts will remember the 1980s as the years of rising
boundary walls in Punjab,' I joked with Jasmeet. The old
mason, down from his perch for lunch, wiped his hands on
his beard and reminded us with a straight face that the sky
would have to be thought of, sooner or later. Every Punjabi,
back in those days, was an expert black humourist. And
a gunman, who cost as much as three doctors at Ahsaas,
manned the gate.

Mundane life plodded on. Antara started going to the
same school as Anhad. I left for work a little earlier and
dropped them on the way. Jasmeet picked them up on her
way back from the clinic. The routine tiptoed on a very
thin ice of sangfroid, below which was a dark lake of fear.
I felt it. Jasmeet felt it. Ma felt it, but never talked about it.
The children sensed it too. Well, they saw the pictures in
newspapers, didn't they? Everybody called it the 'Punjab
Problem', as if it was a stubborn crossword puzzle refusing
to be solved and not a ruthlessly violent terrorist insurgency
in its prime. There were several versions of how it had
started, but many years later, most grandmothers would
tell a story which included 'Dandy' (who dressed in white
and sported a rose to look like Nehru), 'Durga' (who in the
end was slain by the demons) and a fiery 'Priest' bristling
with a long beard and automatic weapons. The Priest was

supposed to be Durga's man, but puffed up, he rebelled, and started a war to get a country of his own, another land of the pure, this time for the Sikhs.

~

I am idly looking out of my office window at Ahsaas, my mind on a news item I have just read in *Prajeet*, the popular Punjabi newspaper. The headline read, 'Learn from Partition and Shift in Time'. It was a short press statement from the Free Homeland Army and said that the time has come for the Sikhs in Punjab to bid farewell to their Hindu brethren and let them go—for their own good! It goes on to advise that lessons should be learnt from 1947. There was a gory reference about trains being meant to carry live people, not dead bodies.

Suddenly I am five years old, shivering in the early morning cold, clutching my father's hand in the crowded vegetable market, while it is still dark. This is the wholesale market, actually a large, open ground, with heaps of vegetables as far as you can see. It comes up only in the morning. You get fresh vegetables at bargain prices straight from the farmers. I am wearing chappals made of tyre rubber. They cut into the skin if one walks fast. I find it difficult to keep up as we abandon one heap of tomatoes for another, my father having failed to bring the first farmer down enough after a hectic round of bargaining. I hear the word 'refugees' hurled at our backs, where it seems to stick—at least to my back. I have heard it at school and, even at five, know that it means people who came here from Pakistan at the time of Partition. But I am still perplexed and so ask, 'How does he know?' My father shrugs his shoulders, shifts the jute bag which is heavy by now, to his left hand, making me run around him, the chappals hurting, to hold his right hand, and says, 'Maybe we bargain too much?'

Whenever Jasmeet has asked me, 'Why don't you ever bargain?' I have always replied flippantly.

Jasmeet is a Sikh and I am not. She now comes into the office, looking for the case file of the schoolgirl who had slashed her wrists on being scolded by the father for coming home late. I look at the maroon bindi on her forehead, which she should not be wearing, since it has been forbidden for Sikh women by a recent diktat for being a Hindu symbol, and ask her, 'Will you sponsor my application for citizenship of the Republic of Khalistan?' She sees the pain in my eyes but pretends otherwise, 'We will see. Some background checks will be required.' She closes the door softly, as if it might crumble.

The door opens again, tentatively, just a few inches, pushed by an intricately hennaed hand and a creamy arm covered with the red and white ivory bangles that newlywed women wear. The bangles clash with the plain white kurta worn by this sobbing bride, who is now clinging to me. I had received her wedding invitation last week, but did not go. I make her sit, give her water and hand her some tissue paper from the box I keep on my table. In between sobs, she tells me that her father Pal Singh, whom I knew longer than her, she being only seventeen, is no more.

Pal, a Punjabi teacher in a village school, got an award
on the last Teachers' Day. I remember him telling me about
it shyly, when he came for his medicines some months ago.
I had stopped at Sanghol once on my way to Ludhiana,
to show Anhad and Antara the site of the Harappan dig
next to Pal's house and the museum which the archaeology
department has on site. The girl, still sobbing, tells me
how Pal had not been going to teach for many days and
refusing medicines too, which he had never done before.
He was upset by the dead bodies turning up regularly on
TV, but he insisted on watching it all day. He would sit
mesmerized with mouth half-open, finding a blown-up
bus here and a charred train there, being shown again and
again until fresh images renewed the endless cycle.

Word had gone around that armed 'boys' were hiding in
the ruins of a temple outside the village. When Pal heard
about it, rage boiled over in his medication-starved brain.
He calmly switched off the TV and, with long flowing hair
and beard, walked past his wife with firm strides. He strode
along the deserted road towards the ruins shouting, 'You
bastards! Call yourselves Sikhs? Found another temple to
hide? Come out if you are real sons of your fathers.' There
is a hint of pride in his daughter's voice as she repeats the
curses, but it soon vanishes in the sobs that accompany
the rest of the story. A hail of bullets from the temple tore
through his chest. The villagers, observing through chinks
in their windows, saw the firing go on long after Pal Singh's
six feet three inches had fallen, making his body twitch
with every burst, in a grotesque parody of life. Motorcycles

revved up behind the temple and roared away. A door burst open and a wailing figure darted across the dim courtyard.

Before leaving, the girl in the mourning clothes keeps a plastic bag softly on the table and says, 'Left-over medicines for poor patients.' She makes an attempt to bend down and touch my feet which I am able to successfully foil, mainly because I had been anticipating it. I look at the armful of red and ivory bangles disappear as she closes the door behind her. Then I empty the plastic bag on the table pretending to rummage through the half-consumed strips of tablets, just so I don't do anything stupid like crying.

~

On Diwali, as always, I keep a watch over the footwear outside the temple, while others go in. The temple loudspeaker, which is way too loud, ensures that the lilting chorus of the aarti is heard, not just by the swaying crowd in the temple courtyard, but by everybody living in the neighbourhood and beyond. The air is rife with smells familiar from childhood. On Diwali, Ma would send me to buy scented incense sticks and I would tear the packet open just a bit and come home sniffing. I look at Ma's flat chappals, Jasmeet's beige sandals with an inch of flat heel, Anhad's black oxfords, a part of his school uniform and, at the end, Antara's pink flip-flops, which she sensibly wears when going to a temple as they are easy to take off and put on.

As my gaze lingers on the tiny flip-flops, a beggar comes up near enough for me to smell the peanuts that he has been eating. His hand goes deep into an inner pocket and comes out with an envelope, which he hands to me, saying, 'Those men gave it for you.' As he turns around to point them out, he looks surprised and then scared. 'They've gone!' he exclaims and hurries away, his eyes troubled. There are already some onlookers.

I slowly walk to the less crowded area at the edge of the compound and look at the envelope in my hand. It has my name written in Gurumukhi. Without opening it, I know what it is. With a steady hand I hold it against the setting sun and carefully tear off the edge. There is a folded letter and two postcard-sized close-ups of Anhad and Antara. Anhad looks sprightly in uniform with the schoolbag strapped to his back. Upright, despite the weight of the schoolbag, he is coming out of the school gate, wearing the same oxford shoes now lying outside the temple. Antara, too, is in her school uniform. Her lips make an 'O' as if she is talking to someone whose face is beyond the edge of the picture. My hands tremble as I unfold the letter.

It is handwritten, a long cursive writing, loops and all, on the official letterhead of the Free Homeland Army. It starts 'Dear Dr Prakash Kohli Sahib, Victory to the Khalsa Panth.' There are a few lines about Dr Kohli being a capable and popular doctor who has been serving Punjab for fifteen years; that was how most such letters started, I had heard. But now, it said, time had come to make some material contribution ('Maya' was the word used) to the ongoing War of Independence. I was lucky to have been selected by the wise men of the council for the honour of contributing forty lakh rupees within a period of fifteen days. The day I was ready to pay, I was to tie a piece of saffron cloth atop the sign saying Armaan on the path which led to my house and wait for a phone call.

The letter warned me about going to the police. 'You have two lovely children and there is no reason other than your stubbornness that they should not live long and happy lives.' The photographs had been taken recently. Anhad still has the scab on his knee visible in the picture. On the reverse of each, their names, class and section numbers, the address of the school and its timings are written neatly in English.

As the four of them come out with vermilion streaks on their foreheads and prasad in their hands, Jasmeet looks perplexed at not finding me guarding the shoes. She turns around in a circle, sees my silhouette against the setting sun at the far end of the compound and begins walking towards me. The music is loud, making any attempt to speak, or even shout, pointless. As she comes near, I say above the din, 'I came here to watch the sunset. Hope the shoes are intact.'

I had been anticipating this. What happened to me ten minutes ago had played out in my mind several times in the recent weeks. It had happened almost exactly the way I had imagined it would, except that it was a postman and not a beggar who was supposed to bring the letter. So when I face Jasmeet, with the crimson horizon now behind her, there is nothing amiss in my expression. On the way back,

I drive calmly, and do not even blink when a cracker hits the bonnet of the car and bursts in front of my face.

I dream that I am ten years old and cycling in the lanes of Amritsar. My feet do not reach the pedals and I am hurtling off balance as if pushed from behind. Then I am cycling with one leg under the bar. I can go fast now, but it suddenly becomes dark and the cycle hits a buffalo lying in the middle of the lane. When I touch it, it is cold steel and not a buffalo at all, but an army tank. A soldier with a helmet is sitting in it. I call out to him, but no voice comes out of my mouth. The soldier does not move because he is dead. When I push back the helmet, I find myself staring at my father's face. I wake with a thumping heart, drenched in sweat. Outside, a firecracker sizzles towards the sky.

'Why didn't you tell me before?' Jasmeet complains, putting the letter and the photos back into the envelope with just the slightest tremor in her hands.

'Did not want to spoil your Diwali,' I say lamely.

An hour later, we decide to inform the police.

~

A month later, as the East Coast Mainline train leaves London's Euston station for Edinburgh, I remember the rude villager selling his heap of tomatoes, the one who had hurled the word 'refugees' perplexing the five-year-old me.

The Nepali guard manning the gate at Ahsaas was shot dead, fifteen minutes after I made a call to the police, telling them about the letter from the Free Homeland Army. I was coming down the stairs and saw the incredulous look on the guard's face as he touched the hole in his chest where he had been shot. As he slumped, I saw the silent blur of a motorcycle through the glass.

The school principal, an impassive nun from Malabar, did not ask any questions, not because she was very discreet, which she was, but because she knew the answers. Anhad and Antara were fetched from their classes. They looked baffled. 'You will be going to a new school in another city. I have been transferred.' I tried to sound cheery and convincing.

'You are lying. You said you cannot be transferred anywhere since you are not in a job!' Anhad was in tears. Antara just clutched my trousers.

'Well, I am transferring myself to another city to build another hospital.' It's the best explanation I could think of. It had taken just an hour to collect papers, certificates, cheque books and clothes, particularly woollens for me. Suresh in Birmingham, who was with us at the Institute, was asked to look for a job for me. Ma was put on a train to Delhi. We were on the platform when she asked me, 'Is it Partition time again?'

I hug her. Feeling her palpitation against my chest, I say, 'Don't be silly. Partitions do not happen every day. We will meet soon.'

Becoming rootless has been easy. It has taken half a day and not even a missed meal, I think to myself, as I recognize Jasmeet's father from his turban in the small crowd outside the airport at Bombay.

At the end of the week, the hospital manager with an MBA from East Anglia calls me to her office and bluntly tells me that there was no need to see extra patients, 'If somebody is seeing more patients than the average, it is a minus, not plus. More is actually less. In the UK, it is all about quality.' I come away hurt and baffled.

Jasmeet keeps me updated about the news from home on a daily basis. She reads out from the *Times of India*, Bombay edition, when I call during my lunch break from the public phone outside the canteen. My pockets are always jingling with coins which I collect obsessively.

'Number of people who died this year was more than in any previous year, Prakash,' she says.

'Yesterday, seventy-five people were shot dead in a train near Ferozepur. It was Christmas day, Prakash.'

'Prakash, thirty-five policemen and their family members were killed in the police colony. Inspector General Gill died, Prakash. You remember we treated his wife.'

~

I take long walks in the Valley Park. I would start around seven in the evening and walk till nine. It has been a long, harsh winter. The snowfall has been bleak. The footpaths are heaped with snow when I leave in the morning. It is dark when I go in for work and darker when I come out.

While looking for Earl Grey tea on the third floor of a supermarket, I see a majestic woman with flaming red hair in a wheelchair, moving playfully through the aisles. She stops suddenly, takes an unexpected turn and disappears for a while, laughing all the time. A handsome man with a drooping moustache, also in a wheelchair, pursues her in the hide-and-seek. I come away quietly, without the tea.

On weekends, the six hours of daylight are dimmed by a featureless grey sky. I wish I did not have to go for work. I find it dull and protocol-driven. Even the manic patients are irritable and not elated. Depressives are listless, bland and bereft of thoughts, even negative. I have become a possessed walker and have this craving to shuffle my legs when I am not walking. Like the bunch of sadhus with plumes stuck in their grubby turbans who used to come and stand, shuffling their feet high up till the knees, clapping their lilting cymbals all the while, till Ma gave them rice.

Months go by. The June sun is harsh, even in the evenings but I don't bother with sunblock cream. When the sunburn on my face heals, thin scales remain. When the scales fall off, there is fresh sunburn.

October. It is midnight and pitch dark on the front lawn as I return from my five-hour-long walk, having lost my way in Holyrood forest. The moment I touch the latch on the gate, I know something is wrong. It has just been left to drop and not pressed down.

'No torch please, Dr Kohli.' Punjabi, conciliatory, meant to put me at ease, but of course having the opposite effect in the inky black darkness. I would have preferred any other language of the world.

'I will be happy to keep your torch.' Firm persuasion from the direction of the wrought-iron bench. The voice is soft. Utterly polite. Somebody who has lived in Yorkshire for years but also speaks an earthy Majha dialect. I extend the torch which is prised out of my hand gently by someone sitting on the bench. I can make out the outlines of a turban but nothing else, except perhaps the hem of a long coat as the man moves. 'Please sit, sir. The chair is right next to you.' I grope with my right hand and find it. The metal feels cold and wet through my flannel trousers.

'My name is not important but I am from the Free Homeland Army.' Then almost apologetically, 'In fact, I am quite high up in the hierarchy. I took over recently.'

All that I can think of at the moment is a wish to be in my bed and asleep. What is the point of anything else? You run to the far corners of the world and they find you the moment they want to.

'I have come to invite you back to Punjab,' the disembodied voice is rather feminine and tantalizingly familiar. I soon get tired of the effort to place it. My calves hurt after the long walk, and a part of my weary mind finds it easier to decide that it is a voice I have never heard before. 'The Council has thought it out. Whosoever rules Punjab, good doctors will be needed...' The voice took on a drone, like a news bulletin. 'There are others who are being contacted. Precautions will still have to be taken to avoid being at the wrong place at the wrong time. Personally, you will not be bothered. Of course, it is optional.'

I have an urge to throw myself bodily at the Sikh, catch him by the throat, and ask if Punjab was his personal courtyard from where people could be thrown out and then invited back. But if it were light, the visitor would not have seen a flicker of expression on my face. Instead, I ask, a little incredulously, 'You came all the way to tell me this?'

'I divide my time between Amritsar and Leeds, so I sort of took it on myself. Now please go in, but do not switch on the lights till I am gone. I am sorry about the funny stuff, but trust me, it is necessary. There was a rustle of a paper being unfolded. 'This, you can have a look at later.'

Once inside, I half-run to the window and pull the edge of the curtain just enough. The silhouette of a stocky man walking with a limp swirls around the corner like a dervish, and is gone. Recognition is slow to come.

* * *

There was a child who sat next to me in the municipal school in Amritsar, on the worn-out strips of jute. You could feel the cool floor through them, which was nice during summer but painfully icy in winter. We all jostled for the thick patches in the winter and the thin ones in summer. He could not run with the others, so I kept his place. He soon left, going back to his uncle in England, everybody said, to be treated for his weak leg and hand. Years later, he reappeared suddenly, one winter afternoon. I was an intern then, in Mental Hospital, Amritsar, sampling Rulda's samosas and chai.

'Is it common in England for a twenty-two-year-old engineer to go on sabbatical?' I asked him. We were sitting on the gurudwara steps, drinking sugarcane juice.

'No, but it is not unheard of either,' Harmohan replied, adjusting his tightly worn saffron turban with one hand and trying to balance the glass with the other. He had an impish smile. 'Beware and be warned, O natives of the Orient. Hundreds of confused teenyboppers from the West unleash themselves to look for solutions to their real, imagined and concocted existential issues.' He winked rakishly.

'Wow. But isn't it a bit early? I mean, you just started your first job,' I said.

'It is never too early. The fact is that most of us who belong neither here nor there are quite messed up, which is fine, because who isn't a little messed up. I mean, those of us who are unlucky enough to know this have a need to sort it out. The insight is very incomplete, so very compelling. Of course, religion is just one of the many ways to go about it. This is what I am giving a trial to, to start with.'

'To start with?' I got up to pay the sugarcane vendor.

'If it does not work in one year, I have a deferred placement in a master's course in philosophy waiting for me at Manchester University. Do I sound crazy?'

We walked down to the corner where we had locked our cycles together, since we had just one chain between us. 'On the contrary; you sound like a good mechanical engineer, trying to use religion as a tool of understanding.' It was not meant to be cynical, but a shadow crossed

Harmohan's face and his limp became more noticeable; when we shook hands soon after, his right hand felt even smaller and softer.

* * *

I switched on the reading light. The paper was a crisp, well-preserved copy of the letter that a beggar had given me last Diwali evening at a crowded Durga temple.

Lying on the bed, even with shoes on, is an ecstatic sensation. The year-long turbulence in my legs was gone. The sadhus had gotten their rice.

SMART ALECK

'You drive very well.' Prakash complimented Mirrat.

'Anybody who lives half the time in Karachi has to. It is a survival thing,' she replied, pulling up neatly in front of the long porch of the station. Mirrat owned a designer boutique in Karachi, which gave her a decent pretext to stay away from Asif whenever the two had too much of each other. Lahore Railway Station looked like a cross between the Old Delhi and Lucknow Charbagh stations. The grand imperial design was the same, but the subdued brick masonry facade set it apart as a sober, more assured cousin. Porters thronged the lawn across the road. The two sets of clocks on the spires told him that his train to Rawalpindi was not due for another twenty minutes. It was not even eleven in the morning, yet the road in front of the station glistened in the heat like a mirage.

'I talk to you because you are a good listener. This doesn't mean that anything has to be done about what I say,' Mirrat said in a distracted manner. She did not seem to be in a hurry to go, now. 'Amber is twelve. She will come home from Murree in six months.' She spoke as if apologizing for her daughter's return from boarding school. 'Tell me. What's your impression? Can things be salvaged? You know him well.'

It was the same question every time they met. And he gave the same answer, 'Yes, if both of you are willing to put in the effort. But I am a friend, and cannot be totally objective.'

This time, Prakash hesitated for a moment but then plunged ahead with the suggestion he'd had in mind since their last meeting. 'What about a marriage counsellor?' he inquired.

'The few that we have in Pakistan are either his cousins or mine. Don't even start about confidentiality and stuff. I think you should start charging me for the amount I talk.'

There was a commotion among the porters and suddenly they sprinted across the road, dodging vehicles. In a few minutes, a steady stream of well-dressed passengers started to emerge from the arches of the cavernous building, many wearing fancy shades and holding their Gucci and Prada handbags. They looked out of place against the groups of dishevelled travellers dotted about the station entrance, squatting or resting their backs against grubby holdalls.

Mirrat glanced at her watch. 'The Allama Iqbal Express has come. It's always on time when I am not travelling,' she said wistfully. A pause, and then, as if there had been no interruption, 'I also talk to you because you are the only person I know who will listen to me and then go away, without lecturing me or him, or making Freddie's Cafe gossip out of it.' Mirrat had this persistent need to explain, as if she thought she was suspected of doing something inappropriate. 'Anyway, off you go now. I don't want anybody to say that I made you miss your train. Thanks for the breakfast,' she neatly changed the subject, decanted him, waved and drove away, weaving through the stream of oversized sedans and SUVs arriving to receive passengers from Karachi.

Two porters came almost running up to him. Prakash waited for the trailing one, a middle-aged man in a long red shirt with rolled-up sleeves, to catch up, and handed him his stroller, 'Rawalpindi Express'. The porter grinned broadly and set off towards the platform.

The train compartment was a row of four-berth cabins with an aisle, very much like air-conditioned coaches in India. There was nobody else in Prakash's cabin, but a water bottle sat on the table and a leather bag on the upper berth. As the train moved out of the station, a tall, thin, rather distinguished-looking man in his sixties entered and nodded to him courteously. It took several minutes to cross the bridge over the Raavi and the booming echo of the iron girders made it difficult to start a conversation. The riverbed below was vast and parched.

As the train slowly ground to a stop at the crowded Shahdara station on the other side of the river, the man unlaced his soft leather shoes, pushed them under his berth and sat cross-legged, his eyes closed. A woman in a burqa with a young boy holding an unopened McDonald's burger peeped in and then stepped back. When the train started again, the two were left sitting facing each other.

The older man opened his eyes and said, 'Now the train will not stop till Gujranwala. Peace for an hour.'

With the ice broken, they discussed each other's professions the way men often do, even before knowing each other's name. The other man was a lawyer and was going to Rawalpindi for a court hearing on behalf of a client. 'And where do you practice, doctor?' he asked.

'I am from India. Here to attend a conference in Rawalpindi,' Prakash said, offering his card.

'I should have guessed that you are from India,' the lawyer rued in a self-deprecating manner, as he returned the courtesy.

Prakash remembered a similar conversation many years ago, with another Pakistani. Ethereally beautiful, razor-sharp, psychiatrist-in-making, journalist and India-baiter Salma Ansari, who said that she could tell an Indian from a Pakistani through the wrong end of a telescope and who, for no fault of her own, was a cause of Mirrat's unhappiness.

'How could you have guessed?' Prakash asked Mr Jaffer Hussain, whose card proclaimed him to be a Barrister-at-Law at the Lahore High Court.

'We speak Punjabi differently now on the two sides. It's possible to make out the difference.... Where are you from in India?' Jaffer asked.

The older people often lost some of their enthusiasm at meeting an Indian on hearing that Prakash lived in Chandigarh. The city was a post-Partition phenomenon. They would have preferred if he were from Amritsar,

Jalandhar or even Ambala. So Prakash said, 'Amritsar, but now I work in Chandigarh.'

As usual, when speaking to someone who might have witnessed the events of Partition, Prakash mentioned his interest in the history of mental hospitals and, particularly, in how hundreds of mental patients were reallocated between the two new countries.

'That sounds fascinating. But are you also aware of a similar exchange of prisoners after Partition?' Jaffer asked.

'Yes, I'd heard that something like that did happen,' nodded Prakash.

'Post-Partition, all prisoners on both sides went through the same process of exchange—except that the numbers of people involved were much higher. The swap happened in 1948, over two phases, in April and October. Around four thousand prisoners went from here to India and an approximately equal number came from there, in trains fortified with bars on the windows,' Jaffer said. 'I know all this because I had a client from the set who came from India.

'O, Waiter-saab!' he interrupted himself, catching sight of a tall man in a turban and green livery. Jaffer ordered tea for both of them.

'I thought people needed lawyers before they were sent to jail, not after,' Prakash said.

'He was not a convicted prisoner. He was an under-trial, charged with murder by the Faizabad police. You know, Faizabad, Uttar Pradesh?'

Prakash nodded.

'Almost half the prisoners who came were under-trials. In fact, most of the Muslim under-trials who were charged with serious offences opted for Pakistan. Many convicted prisoners remained in India,' Jaffer explained.

The tea was brought in an elaborate tea set, complete with a tea cosy made of coarse wool, with the emblem of Pakistan Railways embroidered in green. Prakash offered to pay, knowing well that he would not be allowed to.

'You can pay when I come to Chandigarh, Doctor Sahib,' Jaffer smiled and continued. 'In fact, Ali was an assistant to a lawyer in the Faizabad district courts. He had sound legal advice available to him free of cost while in India.'

'So why did he choose to come to Pakistan? Did he have a relative here?' asked Prakash. He carefully added the thick granulated sugar.

'He did not know a soul here. His father had passed away when he was small. None of his relatives or friends shifted here. He opted for Pakistan based on the legal advice he got. I would have suggested the same.' Jaffer pulled down his leather bag from the upper berth and took out a tin of Mrs Fields cookies. Prakash took two and asked Jaffer, 'Whom did he kill?'

'A colleague, a young man like him, an assistant to another lawyer. It happened in the court premises, in broad daylight, in front of two stamp-paper vendors, right next to the Sessions court. One moment they were shouting at each other, and the next, grappling with drawn knives. Those days, I was told, men routinely carried knives in Faizabad.'

'They still do,' Prakash said. Jaffer did not seem to have heard him.

'By the time the stamp-paper vendors managed to separate them, the other fellow was dying—a wound in the abdomen—while Ali had a slash on his arm. It seemed that the other boy, Irfan, had teased Ali's girlfriend in the bazaar. If I remember correctly—and I could be wrong, because it was a long time back—her name was Mehr,' Jaffer began fussily wiping biscuit crumbs from his shirtfront with a delicately monogrammed handkerchief as he spoke, 'short for Mehrunissa…but like I said, I am not sure about that part. I forget names these days…

'They had been together in school. She came to meet him in jail every other day, without, of course, informing her parents. The jailor was a friend of Ali's boss and let them meet. Ali's application for bail was rejected and the trial date was nowhere in sight. Then came this letter from the Government of India, asking Muslim prisoners whether they would like to stay in India or go to Pakistan. Almost every Muslim man charged with murder or kidnapping opted to go to Pakistan because their lawyers told them that if they went to Pakistan they were certain to be acquitted in the absence of witnesses. The government could not have transported witnesses, along with the accused, could it?' Jaffer asked. Prakash nodded in agreement.

Jaffer looked at his watch and said, 'Please excuse me. It is time for Zuhr. I will be back shortly.' He laced up his shoes and stood up, covering his bald head with an embroidered prayer cap. He turned back at the cabin door and explained, 'There is a vacant cabin at the end of the compartment.' Prakash presumed that was where he had been when the train was starting.

A bustling platform appeared outside the windows and the train stopped. It was Gujranwala, the town where Prakash was born. He remembered Roshaan, the midwife, whose hands had shaken in fear while tying the knot on his belly-button, one riot-torn night, deep inside this city. She lived not far from where he sat. How he wished he had more time on this trip.

He also remembered the drive back from Gujranwala to Lahore in the Impala along with Shaukat, the Lahore student who kept a bottle of Bagpiper whiskey behind his books, and the jeweller brothers, Mehmood and Salman, all of whom he had met at Nankana Sahib. He had met Asif for the first time that evening as well. Since then, he had come to Lahore a few times for medical conferences. Asif made sure that he was invited, since it was as sure a way to get a Pakistani visa as any these days. Often, they travelled together, but this time he had gone ahead a day early, since he was on the organizing committee of the conference.

As the train moved, Jaffer came back with the cap in his hand. He took off his shoes and sat cross-legged again on his berth. There was a faint smell of tobacco in the air.

'And so, a day came in October of '48, when Ali found himself in a makeshift prison in Hissar, along with several thousand other prisoners gathered from jails all over

India, waiting to be transported to Pakistan. The "prison" consisted of hundreds of tents pegged hurriedly in a school ground and surrounded by several layers of barbed-wire fencing. That was the first time that I thought Ali was lying to me: he said that Mehr had come to Hissar to see him off and, according to him, they'd had a long talk across the fence that night. I couldn't believe him, because Faizabad to Hissar is a long, long way, and there was no chance that Mehr's parents would have allowed her to be away alone for two or three days. Ali said he had "managed it", but I think he was so utterly besotted with her that he wanted to carry in his head the romantic notion of farewells across barbed fences. He saw too many war movies, you see.

'I met him at the Central Jail, Lahore. By then, Ali had run out of money. He was not allowed to carry cash, nor did he have a bank account. His trial was not due to start for six months because the process of appointing a government lawyer took time. I had just completed my law degree then and had been assisting a senior lawyer. We were in the court in connection with another case, and the judge was lamenting the fact that two thousand under-trials had been added to the system at one go, most with no lawyers. My senior, without even asking me, yanked me forward, saying that I was willing to be appointed. The judge pushed not one but several files towards me and asked me to meet the court clerk. One of those files was Ali's.

'He was almost as old as me and very impatient to get out. He'd been under the impression that he would be set free as soon as he reached Pakistan. I explained the procedure to him. His file contained sworn statements from the two stamp-paper vendors who had seen the scuffle. I argued before the court that the statements had no evidentiary value unless the defence had an opportunity to cross-examine the witnesses. I convinced the judge to send them summons on our behalf at their Faizabad addresses, saying that we will organize their permits and pay for the travel. They were Hindus and everybody knew that they would not come. When nobody either wrote or turned up for three consecutive hearings, Ali was acquitted.'

The train was now crossing a river full of swirling water flowing just a few feet below the mile-long bridge. 'Chenab,' offered Jaffer as an explanation. Then, 'Have you read Sohni-Mahiwal?'

Prakash nodded. Part of the folklore in both Indian and Pakistani parts of Punjab, the legendary love story had Sohni swimming across the swollen Chenab every night to meet her lover, Mahiwal. He'd known it all his life, and was more interested in the recently acquitted prisoner's tale. 'What did Ali do after that?'

'By then, he'd been allowed to open a bank account, and had some money which he said had been sent by Mehr— her father was apparently a well-to-do cloth merchant in Faizabad. So, Ali hired a room near Lohari Gate and started haunting the Indian Consulate. He insisted on paying rent on a weekly basis, since he was sure that he would return to Faizabad before the month was out. That month went by and nothing happened. Then somebody advised him that he was in the wrong city. Karachi was the capital then, and that is where the Indian High Commission was. The Lahore office had limited powers, he was informed.'

Jaffer turned towards the cabin door and yelled for the waiter again. 'I am hungry. So should you be. They serve divine mutton biryani here. You are not a vegetarian, I hope, because that is all they have for lunch.' He seemed to be a frequent traveller on the train.

Over lunch, Jaffer did not talk about Ali. Instead, he talked animatedly about the cricket match that Pakistan and India were to play the next day in Abu Dhabi. The average Pakistani knew more about cricket than Prakash, although he did follow cricket. Even Mirrat knew all about seamers and off-spinners. He asked, 'So, what's your prediction for the match?'

'You will win. Your new bowler, Kumble—he's deadly.'

Jaffer did not let Prakash pay, saying again, 'Doctor Sahib, you can pay as much you want when I come to India. I promise that I won't stop you.' He kept his wallet on the tray table. Prakash saw that it had a young girl's photo in the clear plastic flap usually used for business cards.

'Pretty girl. Your daughter?' asked Prakash.

'No. I'm not married. Never was.' Jaffer said curtly. He folded the wallet and pushed it into his shirt pocket as if not wanting to pursue that line of conversation. There was a pause.

The train crossed another long bridge over a brimming river and then stopped at a platform. The crowd had a sprinkling of army men with steel trunks waiting to board the train. 'Jhelum.' Jaffer said. 'A million rupees a month wouldn't make me live here. It gets flooded every few years.'

'So did you meet Ali again after he left Lahore?' Prakash asked.

'For six months, he was in Karachi. Then, one day, he turned up in my cabin in the district courts, looking like a scarecrow. He was always thin, yet he seemed to have lost a lot of weight. His face was dark and pinched as if he had been in the sun a lot.' Jaffer was back in flow as a raconteur, sitting with a hand cupping his cheek. The train glided out of Jhelum Railway Station.

'The clerk at the Indian High Commission had told him acidly, "You were asked by the Indian government politely, and you said you wanted to go to Pakistan. You were brought here on government expense. It has not been a year and now you say you want to visit India. India is not a company bagh where you can go for a walk whenever the fancy strikes you."

'After that, God knows how, within a month Ali produced a medical certificate from a Faizabad doctor saying that his mother was on the verge of death and wished to meet him before she died. The clerk threw it back in his face saying that the name of Ali's mother could not be Kamla—a Hindu name. He threatened that Ali could be sent to jail all over again for submitting a false certificate. He and the peon actually dragged Ali to the senior officer's room. But Ali begged and swore that his mother's name was Amla, and that this was an honest mistake by the busy doctor. The only concession he received was that the High Commission agreed not to inform the police, if Ali himself tore the certificate up in front of them. Ali tearfully did so.

'But in another month he was back before the clerk with another certificate, this time in the name of Amla, held between his folded palms. The High Commission took another month, but finally did give him a permit to visit India for six weeks. He boarded the Karachi–Jaipur train and was allowed to cross without any problem by the Pakistani immigration officers at Khokrapar. However, at Munabao, the first station on the Indian side, the immigration inspector informed him that the whole permit system had been discontinued by both the governments as of three days ago. Now, the only valid document permitting entry into India for Pakistanis would be an Indian visa on a Pakistani passport.'

The train had stopped for some reason, their compartment stuck on a bridge high above a seasonal rivulet, the water hurtling frothily down a slope. The sun was still high above the stretch of low hills which formed the horizon now.

'So Ali had come to you for help with the passport?' Prakash hazarded.

'Yes. For the second time, he told me something outlandish. I thought that he had finally gone round the bend–' Jaffer was interrupted by a long whistle, and the train started to move again. A bunch of dark purple flowers brushed firmly against the window pane.

He resumed, 'Ali said that at Munabao railway station,

he met Mehr, who had come to receive him. He said that the officer let them sit together in the waiting room for a couple of hours before he was led away. He was officially deported aboard the same train on its return journey. I told him that I did not believe that part. It was like his yarn about Mehr having come to see him off at Hissar and the two of them having had that romantic farewell at night across the barbed wire fence, all moonshine. Ali insisted that she looked exquisite in her black shirt and sharaara. He said she was in mourning because her mother had passed away.'

Barracks, low buildings with sloping green roofs standing in long rows, started coming into view. On both sides of the track were open grounds, with army trucks parked end to end. A buzz of activity in the corridor outside the cabin hinted that the train was nearing its destination. The woman in the burqa and the young boy passed the cabin again, dragging a duffel bag.

'So did Ali get the passport?' Prakash asked.

'No, not in time... His having being in prison was an issue. Although he had been acquitted, the state technically could still have appealed to a higher court and that was a hurdle. They had absolutely no intention of doing any such thing in his, or in hundreds of similar cases, but it was not possible to get a document saying so before a mandatory period had passed. He did get a passport after a year's wait. But it was useless for him, because the Indian High Commission refused him a visa on the grounds that he had been deported from the country.

'Meanwhile, Mehr's father had had enough. She was already twenty-three, and he married her off to a cloth merchant's son in Dubai. I used to see Ali, but have not met him for a very long time now...' Jaffer stretched his arms, stifling a yawn. He pulled forward the shoes with the tips of his toes and squeezed his feet in. 'Many exchanges happened at the time of Partition, Doctor Sahib. It is time to move on. It has been a long time, a whole lifetime.'

Prakash looked at Jaffer, who had taken out a Jinnah cap from his bag and was adjusting it on his head before the mirror, and asked gently, in a low voice, 'That photograph in your wallet Mr Hussain, she is Mehrunissa, no?'

Jaffer turned around sharply and glared down at Prakash. He sat on his berth, put his head back and with eyes closed, spoke quietly, 'How did you know?'

'I didn't know for certain. I just became curious when you hemmed and hawed too much about not being sure about Mehr's name,' Prakash explained sheepishly. 'I could have been wrong, but then the way you reacted when I asked if the photo in your wallet was your daughter...' He was wondering what had come over him and why could he not have gone on to attend his conference without knowing for sure whether Ali and Jaffer were the same person.

Jaffer picked up his water bottle from the table and took a long gulp. Then he sat up and began speaking in short, sharp sarcastic bursts, in complete contrast to his earlier manner. 'So you are very smart, no, Dr Prakash Kohli, psychiatrist and all? You can read people's minds?

Tell me, could you also have guessed that on the fateful day I had that fight in Faizabad, I was a Saryuparin Brahmin? Did you know that my name was Ram Avtar Mishra and I lived in Ayodhya, which was next door? Or that I worked in Faizabad, where Mehr lived? Could you have guessed that my mother's name was Kamla after all?'

Prakash sat listening impassively. He sensed there was more to come.

'Some days after I was arrested, the government asked all the Muslim prisoners, "India or Pakistan?" The lawyer whom I worked for went to the Imambara mosque and procured a certificate dated eight months before, saying that Ram Avtar Mishra had converted to Islam, of his free will, and had been re-named Jaffer Hussain.' He was speaking more calmly now, caught again in the spell of the past. 'Of course, I did very much think that this would please Mehr and her parents no end. I thought I was being a smart aleck, killing two birds with one stone... I hate smart alecks now.

'Of course, there is also an equally strong possibility that I might have made all this up just now, only to spite you for having guessed correctly the first time.' Jaffer grinned at Prakash, sitting there. 'I'm a lawyer—supposed to think on my feet. Now go home and figure this out,' he finished, then held out his hand in a conciliatory gesture. The train had entered a railway station so crowded with army men there to receive their officers that the scene seemed right out of a Wehrmacht war movie. They shook hands, and moved down the corridor.

As Prakash put his attaché case down on the platform to look around for Asif, an army band started playing in front of the next compartment. Jaffer walked towards him with his own bag, and said above the din, 'I'm sorry, but I have to take back my prediction about tomorrow's match. India will lose,' he said gleefully. 'The waiter just heard on the radio that Kumble has hurt his finger during net practice and won't be playing tomorrow.' Prakash saw the twinkle in his eyes before he disappeared behind a row of olive-green uniforms.

THREE PASSPORTS

The visa officer at the Indian High Commission in London finally looked up from the blue, green and wine-red passports spread out on the table. He contemplated the three of us sitting in front of him and, to our relief, grinned broadly, 'What a fascinating family! Three different citizenships in a family, and those Indian, Pakistani and British. Wow, you've made my day!'

Anhad, having decided that it is genuine amazement and not a wisecrack, smiled back. Anhad, of course, hadn't come for his own visa. He'd brought his passport to support our visa applications. The officer looked at almost-three-year-old Sehrish sitting primly in a low chair, and said, 'Madam Sehrish Siddique Kohli will have no problem. We give visitors' visas to UK citizens all the time.'

Looking at me, he continued, 'Mrs Kohli, beg your pardon, Ms Siddique, your application will go to Delhi and will have to be cleared from there. Pakistani citizens have to apply at least three months in advance for family visas.

'However,' he looked around as if all of us, including him, were a bunch of scheming kids, 'as a doctor, if you were attending a conference in India and had a sponsorship from the organizers, it would be an entirely different matter. It seems to be the only way, if Diwali is when you want to be there. Your passport would still have to go to Delhi though.' It was mid-October already. Diwali was three weeks away.

We returned to our hotel near Hyde Park and Anhad called his father in Chandigarh to tell him about the unusual advice from the visa officer. Prakash simply said, 'Do-able. As it happens, this is conference season. Give me till tomorrow morning, our time, and I'll get an invitation for Saba.'

* * *

While being pulled by Sehrish in the direction of the ice-cream cart and by Anhad towards the lake-front bar, I looked fondly at his long hair tied into a neat ponytail and remember how we had met each other four years ago.

It was my very first Diwali party. I was the only Pakistani there, although the town of Chester and the hospital had more than their fair share. I hoped the hosts would introduce me to the gorgeous tall boy with long hair, even if he was likely to be an Indian, but the Desais were in the kitchen organizing drinks and snacks. I need not have worried. He inched closer to the group I was in, as I answered the usual questions about my identity. 'I'm actually a Punjabi, but was born in Hyderabad. Parents were bureaucrats, so I got to romp all over the country.'

He said hello to somebody he knew. The circle politely expanded to include him. 'I am from Chandigarh. I overheard that you are from Punjab…' I knew what was coming. Partly it was the sari I was wearing that day, and partly that the Greek god had appalling general knowledge. 'Which place exactly?'

'Lahore. From the other Punjab. In Pakistan,' I replied in Punjabi, emphasizing the word 'other', thoroughly enjoying the expressions on his face. Teasing Indians was a thing with me.

'But you said you were born in Hyderabad,' he pointed out, somewhat combatively.

'So I did, but where is the problem? You think that you Indians have a monopoly over the name Hyderabad? There is a Hyderabad in Sind province, didn't you know? You should look at maps more often,' I advised. 'Watch some Pakistani movies too.'

'When you see a Punjabi girl wearing a sari, at a pre-Diwali party hosted by Gujaratis, and the girl says she was born in Hyderabad, one has a right to be confused if it turns out that she is from Pakistan,' he argued. Then he smiled. It brought up crinkles around his eyes. He said, 'Didn't know there were Pakistani movies.'

'Oh, an Indian with a sense of humour! Is your monopoly extended to saris too?' This would have gone on, but the Desais came by and we were introduced, 'Saba, Anhad, both of you are in Psychiatry, Anhad in Liverpool, Saba here.'

I was in a forgiving mood. Besides, I am all for funny jibes. 'Never mind, it has happened before.'

We met a few times. There were many things we had

in common, including psychiatry and a penchant for long walks. We wandered around the cobbled streets and sat talking at the city wall. On Saturdays, we drove into Wales and went hiking. We studied together, discussed our patients, and had heated arguments, bordering on quarrels.

Six months later, both of us had passed the first of the two examinations for the membership to the Royal College of Psychiatrists. But our relationship refused to move forward, as if tied to a rock at the bottom of the river. The talks were intellectual and the jokes were not getting any better. Squash was just an exercise and hiking simply involved not talking for miles, while carrying heavy backpacks.

It was a formless thing that was bogging us down. As we spent more time together, it arranged itself into a shrill set of questions in my head. One evening, we sat discussing Jung outside a Turkish restaurant on the riverside in Liverpool. I had to submit an assignment on his theories. It was a breezy day and the Mersey was dotted with colourful steamers, bobbing up and down as the wind freshened and died. 'It is eerie to know that the way I feel and behave has a stamp, even if in a small measure, of what our prehistoric ancestors felt when they saw a thunderbolt hit a tree,' Anhad was saying, his long hair all over his face.

'I don't see anything strange there. It actually sounds logical. Otherwise, how would one explain why the symbols used by tribes in Australia five thousand years ago are similar to the totems of primitive communities in other continents?'

Anhad looked intently at me as I talked animatedly. 'All right, I cannot handle it anymore,' he put his hands on mine.

'Let's talk about the elephant in the room,' I agreed.

He hesitated. 'The bottom-line is that we love each other. Okay?'

I burst out laughing because he said it so lamely. 'Not okay. The bottom-lines keep changing. Right now, there are issues bigger than the two of us…at least so it seems.'

'Like what?' Anhad asked, even though I was sure that he knew what I was going to talk about.

'Like religion.' I said raising my voice over the wind. I wondered if it had come out too loud.

'We keep our religions,' Anhad replied. 'You carry on being a practising Muslim, and I carry on being a non-practising Hindu. You remain Saba Siddique because she is the one I love.'

'Your smart-ass answers just play havoc with my anxieties.' I said, again raising my voice to compete with the breeze which, perversely, suddenly fell away. I felt unsure and all awkward, as if I was making mountains out of molehills. But the weight of the rock was still between us.

'I am ready with the answers because I've thought them through. Please don't mistake clarity of mind for frivolity.' He looked hurt. I wondered if we were going to quarrel. Maybe we should return to the conversation later. But the talkative parrot sitting within me spat out another question:

'What would be the children's religion?' and I added as if to justify the question, 'My parents are going to ask.' Why did I have to add that?

'I don't come into it. It will be between you and the prospective children. And before you ask, my parents won't have anything to do with it. I know them. It is actually weird, but that is the way they are.'

'So I stay Muslim. Children can go to a mosque? Right?' I had this senseless, visceral need for assurance.

'Right. I even promise to organize halaal stuff. Happy?' I gave him a hard look, decided that he was serious, and ticked off the list of questions in my head to get to the last one.

'Do you know where can one get halaal condoms?' I saw Anhad trying to suppress that crack but he couldn't. He pulled at his ear sheepishly as a motorboat backfired in the distance, drowning out my own spluttering.

'If you can stop being funny, tell me how do we handle the visa thing? I mean, after we are married and if we go to Chandigarh for a vacation, I can't just decide on a whim to go to Lahore and meet my parents over the weekend, even if it is just a few hours away.'

He got exasperated at that, 'Some issues will remain. Nobody has a perfect life.'

It started to rain. By the time we reached the parking lot, we were drenched and laughing crazily. Anhad sank to his knees next to the car and with rain lashing his upturned face, asked, 'Saba Siddique, will you marry me?'

That night, we studied till late and slept on the carpet,

surrounded by a jumble of books, laptops, cell phones, chargers and clothes.

* * *

In the afternoon, the fax machine behind the reception counter at the hotel, prodded to life by our collective stares, spewed out a sponsorship form in the name of Dr Saba Siddique of Liverpool, from the organizing committee of the annual conference of the Indian Psychiatry Society (North Zone) at Jalandhar on November 6. When we showed up at the embassy with the next morning, the visa officer was surprised and impressed, 'Fast work. It will still take two weeks. It is three weeks to Diwali, so it should be fine, no?'

Sehrish's passport was returned to us with a visa stamp in it. Since my visa had the possibility of getting delayed, Anhad and Sehrish would book their tickets to Delhi and go ahead. After I got the visa, I would first go to Lahore, meet my parents, and then cross into India at Wagah. Jalandhar was just an hour's drive from there. On the visa officer's advice, I submitted a separate application for permission to cross the border 'on foot'.

The next morning, the three of us were again sitting in a line before a visa officer, this time at the High Commission of Pakistan, to apply for Sehrish's visa. Anhad had to apply for his visa at the Pakistani High Commission in New Delhi. He had come to the UK a year after me and was not a permanent resident there.

'With three different citizenships and such complicated

itineraries, we need a full-time travel agent just for our family,' Anhad quipped on the train back to Liverpool.

~

In Lahore, my father saw my passport and informed me cheerfully that the visa was valid just for Jalandhar and I couldn't go to Chandigarh. 'India and Pakistan issue city-specific visas to each other,' he said. 'If the two governments could, they would narrow it down to specific buildings. You'll need a separate permission for Chandigarh.' That resulted in a flurry of desperate calls between me and Anhad in Chandigarh.

Later, I asked my father the bureaucrat, 'Sir, how many permissions does one need to meet one's husband?'

He served sharply across the badminton net, 'That question should have been asked before you went and married a bloody Indian! Couldn't you manage an Indian Muslim at least?' he asked sweetly. Not for the first time.

~

Just a couple of hundred kilometres across the border on the Indian side, Anhad was entertaining an unexpected visitor in his parents' drawing room. The visiting card had read, 'Balwant Bharti, Inspector, Intelligence Bureau, Ministry of Home Affairs'. The Inspector was a stocky man, carrying a briefcase which had seen better days. From it, he produced a brown file filled with papers held down by a metal clasp. He also took out several computer printouts, thickly covered with rows of minuscule typeface. He had come to investigate why, in just three days, ninety-four calls had been made to Pakistan, and forty-two received on a cell phone in this house. The printouts were the details of the calls. The Inspector apologized after every sip of tea and explained that it was a mere formality; that 'over-use spikes' were investigated as a matter of course. Anhad had never heard of the term.

The Inspector regretted that he was causing inconvenience on a Sunday but went on to insist that 'rules are rules'. 'After all, Pakistan is an enemy country, sir.' He mentioned that he knew the 'elder doctor sahib' very well because his wife had been treated by him three years ago. 'But a file's belly needs to be filled, sir.'

He wanted a copy of Anhad's passport 'even if it is Indian'. This was given. He also wanted a copy of 'Sehrish Baby's passport, including the visa page, please. Is it a new name?' Anhad ignored the question and gave him the document.

Before leaving, he also wanted to have a look at Anhad's cell phone. 'Beautiful gadget. Rather big for a cell phone. I hope this is not a satellite phone, sir, because those are not allowed.' Anhad explained that it was a cell phone and data organizer, which was why it looked bigger. Half an hour later, still muttering apologies, the detective left, satisfied with his investigations but still perplexed about why Dr Prakash Kohli's son would go and get married to a Pakistani Muslim girl.

~

Anhad had been waiting for an hour on the Indian side of Wagah border, he told me later. He could not call me as cell phones did not work there. The Indian government had put jammers in place to make it difficult for opium smugglers to arrange pick-ups. The whole area was heavily barricaded. He was the only person waiting. I was probably the only person crossing that day. Both countries issued visas stingily—forty per week would be an overestimate. The Punjab Police, Border Security Force, Immigration and Customs authorities, all had a heavy presence on both sides of the border. It seemed incongruous that all this was for just one person that day.

I saw him first. He was wearing a blazer with a college insignia which I had not seen before. Porters, drivers, policemen and security personnel, Customs officers, all stared at me, the only traveller from the 'other side' as I crossed the opening in the barricade. It seemed so bleak and lonely, despite all the security.

After an hour's drive, we were in Jalandhar. Anhad drove to the sprawling conference venue where colourful banners welcomed the delegates. As we checked in, the elderly Sikh receptionist noticed him hesitating at the column on the hotel form demanding citizenship. He asked, 'Is there a problem, sir?'

I replied, 'I am the problem. I am a Pakistani. He is an Indian. Do I need to fill a separate form?'

'Welcome to India. Actually, yes, you do. I will need your passport too.'

After adjusting his glasses and reading the visa stamp, he said, 'Your visa requires you to obtain a police verification every day.' None of us were remotely aware of this. When I asked him if I needed to go to the police station for the verification, he held up his hand reassuringly, saying, 'Technically yes. But if you leave your passport with me, the hotel will get it done for you. We will verify that you are staying with us.' He added, 'My daughter looks like you.'

'Okay. What does she do?' I was warming up to him.

'Picks oranges in California. She is not legal yet. Her aunt took her there.'

Anhad, feeling left out, said, 'She is my wife.'

'Then you must be living abroad, because it would not be easy for you to live together, either here or in Pakistan.'

'We live in England. We are here for the conference,' I gestured to the banners in the lobby. 'Then we go to Chandigarh to be with my in-laws for Diwali.' While Anhad continued to pen in the details for both our forms, I chatted as if he were an an old schoolmate.

'But your visa is only for Jalandhar.' It was probably his job to guide people, but I was taken aback, after his helpfulness about the police check-ins. Anhad looked up from the form that he was filling and interjected, 'We have applied for Chandigarh too. It will come through by tomorrow, hopefully.'

'Visas between India and Pakistan are fickle creatures. They often do not turn up,' the receptionist cautioned him.

Before filling in the 'Number of Days of Stay', Anhad paused and glanced up at the receptionist, who gave a barely perceptible nod. He wrote 'Four'. I thought we were leaving for Chandigarh the next morning, but kept quiet. We went out to the car and Anhad took out his overnight bag. By now I was quite agog at this clandestine conspiracy and didn't ask why my attaché case was left behind in the car.

We went to the convention centre at the other end of the hotel and got ourselves registered for the conference. According to the printed programme, a session on Autism should just have started. At the end of it, I asked a few questions and all heads turned to identify the new voice. By dinner, we had met everybody and thanked the host for inviting us on such short notice.

Anhad woke me up at four and whispered as if we were planning a robbery, 'Let's go to Chandigarh.'

We both used Anhad's toothbrush. I continued wearing his kurta-pyjama but he wore a fresh shirt and trousers. The clothes from the previous day were left hanging in the cupboard, above Anhad's bag. My cell phone remained on the table in silent mode, attached to its charger. Our room was on the first floor, and we took the nearby stairs. There was nobody at the reception.

The car entered the wicker gates of Armaan at seven-thirty in the morning. I loved the driveway, almost carpeted with a thick layer of fragrant harsingar flowers. The overhanging branches scraped the windscreen. It was like entering a living tunnel. Sehrish was at the door with her grandparents, asking, 'Why are you wearing Papa's night dress?'

Over breakfast, Prakash said, 'At least you met nice folks at both the High Commissions. That is not the usual experience. Normally they compete with each other to be nasty. The two countries were born together, and even at the ripe old age of seventy, they show sibling rivalry that, in eight-year-old boys, would be akin to pissing matches to decide whose stream goes farther. Some years ago, I organized a conference and colleagues from Pakistan were to participate. The Joint Secretary in Delhi held on to the visa clearance till the very last minute—he only gave it when he knew it was too late for the delegates from Pakistan to travel. When I asked him on phone, "Aap aisa kyun karte hain?" he shot back, "Woh bhi to aisa hi karte hain".'

Anhad had told me there were long rows of unwashed men, women and children outside the Pakistani High Commission in Delhi, who had been coming there for months, in the hope of a visa—a chance to meet their wives, husbands, children, parents or siblings on the other side of the border. They were not likely to receive an invitation to any conference in Lahore, as Anhad had, thanks to my father's golfing connections. Another conference where we would register ourselves, but not attend.

~

The next day, there was a Diwali mela at Anhad's old school in the evening, so we decided to walk down as a family and visit the school earlier in the afternoon. We met his kindergarten teacher, who was now the Principal. Anhad recognized the short, slim woman in a religious habit with a thick cross, and went up to greet her. With a sharp look through her thick glasses, she placed him immediately and they were soon in conversation about Antara's recent visit. She told me that his naughtiness gave her more trouble than rest of the class put together. Since I seemed to have tamed him—and since I was a child psychiatrist—would I please give a talk to the teachers in her school later in the day about how to manage hyperactive children? Although it was a holiday, all the teachers lived in the convent and would be happy to come.

We went on a tour of the school, winding up in a classroom overlooking a vast playground, with the Shimla hills on the distant horizon—Anhad's classroom in Standard Six. Anhad and Sehrish sat among the audience of nuns, and I delivered an impromptu lecture on adolescent and childhood behaviour. There were many questions, and in the end I was presented with a school shield, otherwise awarded to outstanding students at the annual School Day. 'I was here for eight years and never got that,' Anhad said enviously.

We returned in the evening for the mela, after Sehrish's bedtime. I wandered around, buying gifts for my parents, and admiring the rangolis drawn by students. When I turned back, I found Anhad talking to a stocky man, with a rather plump wife, carrying shopping bags in both her hands, preoccupied with the antics of her ten-year-old twins, as they buzzed between the stalls. The man was introduced to me as Mr Balwant Bharti, and I to them as Mita Kohli, Anhad's cousin from Hyderabad.

'What was that about?' I asked, bewildered, as we turned away after exchanging pleasantries.

'He's an IB Inspector and a paranoid one. Doesn't like Pakistan, and knows that I'm married to a Pakistani.'

'But why tell so many lies…'

'He may have asked to see your passport—which is in Jalandhar. You aren't supposed to be here either…. And anyway, you *are* from Hyderabad, aren't you?' he added, grinning.

A SPY NAMED GOPAL PUNJABI

Samiullah Ahmed Pasha—'Sami' to his former colleagues in the Inter-Services Intelligence agency—rises from his seat as his stop comes up on the display. Ignoring the bus conductor's hand stretched out helpfully, he gets down lightly at the corner of G-7. He prefers to walk the rest of the distance, along a broad avenue lined with amaltas trees to the far corner of a sprawling block, in what is arguably the most uptown location in Islamabad.

If he feels any degree of self-consciousness, walking in the classy neighbourhood in his faded long shirt and tucked-up salwar which shows his calloused ankles, he displays no sign of it. In fact, he walks rather cockily. After all, the building he is heading to had been his workplace for many years and he has been coming here every month to collect his pension. Not to mention being called in once in a while to be briefed for some extra work. That bonus exceeds his pension several times over. It is paid to him in cash straight from a steel cupboard by the senior cashier. Sami knows that he is summoned for certain niche jobs because he is a specialist. His age is a plus point. It makes him look innocuous at immigration counters. He is also realist enough to know that it is simpler for the agency to disown a former officer than an active one, if an operation in a foreign country blows up in their face.

The spy headquarters is the last building on the street, where the elegant avenue joins a highway which skirts a panoramic lake, before heading north-east to Azad Kashmir. The majestic edifice, painted in a soothing beige colour, looks more like a well funded library, with its sprawling lawns and fountains, than the nerve-centre of one of the most feared spy organizations in the world. With its high, domed glass lobby easily visible from the road, it appears to be a shining symbol of transparency. However, everybody seems to know that all it takes for bombs to go off in distant marketplaces, is a man on the top floor picking up a phone. So people, even the ones who are not aware of snipers on the roofs and of barriers, soldiers and sniffer dogs behind the lobby, discreetly stay away. The vast avenue remains deserted, even during the day.

For Sami, it is a matter of less than an hour before he is back at his stop, waiting for the return bus to Rawalpindi just fifteen kilometres away. He has the neatly folded pension cheque in his wallet and carries a paper bag from Subway, which had contained a sandwich for the cashier earlier, and now holds his bonus. He carries it, slung casually, in the crook of his little finger, like someone used to carrying cash around all his life. Five lakh rupees for two days' work, even in the miserably snowed-in city of Mazar-e-Sharif in North Afghanistan, is not bad work for a sixty-eight-year-old spy, Sami thinks. He admires his reflection smugly in the bus driver's mirror, his henna-coloured beard, hurriedly shaven upper lip and the bald head covered with a skull cap crocheted by Aalia.

~

The two days had been spent in the company of an Indian in the same trade. He should ideally have been cremated, not buried, but then, such were the exigencies of Sami's profession.

~

On seeing a girl with a school bag and a bouncy ponytail get on the bus at the Burma Town crossing, he suddenly remembers that he had promised his grandchildren the story of Gopal Punjabi, the fabled spy, for tonight. When he'd suggested telling another spy story since he did not know all the details about this one, Huma had insisted it had to be Gopal Punjabi. It was his own doing. He had once boasted to the children that he knew Gopal Punjabi very well. He'll have to tailor the tale, he thinks. While grandfathers, even those who have been spies, have the right to tell stories of their colleagues' adventures—or even of their own—to their grandchildren, the Official Secrets Act is not to be scoffed at. Precautions have to be taken even thirty years after the death of the protagonist—particularly since children are apt to boast in school. While there is no law against spinning fictional narratives to spice up a story session, telling the whole truth is quite another matter.

Sami leaves the bus at the railway workshop stop and takes a long detour, via the washing lines where the green and yellow compartments of an endlessly long train are being pressure-hosed by men in blue. At Ganj Mandi, he orders tea at a small eatery right opposite a school. He often spends hours there, doing nothing, feeding the overweight parrot in the cage hanging over the entrance, reading a newspaper, idly looking out of the window. Half an hour later, the school bell shrills and he waits for the curly-haired six-year-old to come out and be hugged and carried away by his father, a clean-shaven young man, to a waiting motorbike, the child giggling with pleasure all the time. Sami does not know either the child or the father.

As the afternoon sun lengthens the shadows, Sami turns into the bustling maze of lanes behind Raja Bazaar, full of colourful fruit carts, tinkling bicycles, noisy hawkers and persistent beggars. Deep inside, where two lanes cross, he lives in a spacious house, the ground floor of which has several shops, like a mini-market. His hard-earned money, well invested, all in all, Sami has done well for himself. The newly bought Suzuki Mehran is parked neatly in the lane below his house, which means Aalia has fetched the kids from school. The driver would be smoking around the corner, in front of the girls' madrassa. He must dismiss him before Huma grows up, Sami thinks with a twinge of grandfatherly anxiety.

Salman, the boy in the grocery shop says an enthusiastic salaam to him. The paan shop tenant, Faraz, who is behind with the rent, is even more exuberant. The garbage bin in the corner has not been cleaned, judging by the number of stray dogs circling it. Sami gives a piece of his mind to the butcher, its main contributor. He has no hesitation in threatening his errant tenants with being hung upside down over a burning furnace, although he never mentions the letters ISI. Well, if they know anyway, what can he do about it? The tenants on their part also know how the previous owner of the building who had been reluctant to sell, (although his alcoholic son had been keen), had disappeared without a trace—but then that was just hearsay, and decades ago, before any of them were even born.

Mina, who managed the ladies' salon, grins naughtily at him from inside the shop. Sami smiles with his face down and keeps walking without breaking pace, the Subway bag dangling from his fingers. He is late and Aalia would be watching from the window. He had not even called. He looks at his watch and decides to join the afternoon Asr prayer at the mosque.

Since the Imam is away with fever, Sami is asked to lead the prayer. It is another hour before he returns and climbs the stairs, first carefully inspecting the parked Mehran. It is not his first car, but Sami is a hypochondriac when it comes to cars. He worries that the air in the rear tyres is low and reminds himself to tell the driver about it. By the time he reaches the top of the stairs, he's short of breath and gropes for the small vial of angina tablets in his pocket. But the distress passes off as soon as his bulk settles in the reclining chair. He hands over the paper bag to Aalia without comment from either of them, eats some of the biryani that she brings and promptly falls asleep in the chair.

He dreams of a helicopter hit by a missile, landing askew in a blizzard of snow, men shooting at each other, streams of blood seeping into fresh snow. Sami awakes, startled. He realizes that what had actually woken him up was Huma and Saqib's quarrelling in the next room over a game of carrom. Saqib had slyly pocketed two of his own pieces when a trusting Huma had gone to the kitchen to get him a glass of water.

Sipping tea, but without moving from the chair, he asks in the direction of the kitchen, 'Did Rehman or Zeba call?' Their son and daughter-in-law telephoned twice a week— Sundays and Wednesdays. Rehman was a Major stationed in Azad Kashmir, near the Indian border.

'The connection was bad. And there has been firing for three days; two men died, five hurt,' Aalia replies, her voice heavy with anxiety. 'Our President says he will work for peace.'

'Peace my foot. Will he go with the mushy peaceniks to light candles at Wagah border? Those kaffirs understand just one language—that of nukes. We should drop a big one on Srinagar, take the rest of Kashmir and finish the matter once for all.'

'If we drop a "big one", what will be left there to take? And won't they drop a bigger one on Isloo?' Aalia reasons. They go on to discuss the pros and cons of another war with India and the geopolitics of the subcontinent for another half an hour, branching out into the two-nation theory, selfish Americans, corrupt ministers and girls being allowed to wear jeans by godless parents. All the while, Aalia rolls chapattis for the four of them, the rogan josh having been already cooked by the maid. They stop only when the kids ask Aalia when they could talk to their parents, although they knew the answer will be 'Sunday'. Sami smokes his only cigarette of the day, though he is not supposed to have even that.

During dinner, the kids continue to quarrel about what to watch on TV. Sami is lulled into thinking that the storytelling session has been forgotten. The two settle on *Alpha Bravo*, a serial about the military. As the episode ends and a cheery lassi commercial comes on, Huma, who'd been helping Aalia remove the plates quickly, asks Sami upfront, looking right into his eyes, 'Was Gopal Punjabi his real name?'

Sami pulls a stool forward to rest his feet, swollen from his travels. With the TV switched off, Aalia cleaning up in the kitchen but well within earshot, and Huma and Saqib sitting at the edge of the sofa, it is story time. Settling back in the chair, he sighs, 'Unlikely. If a spy is good, nobody knows his real name…and he was one of the best.'

'What was your name when you were in Jakarta?' Saqib asks, deadpan.

'Muhammad Suharto,' Sami replies, equally deadpan. This was a game the two often played, varying the name of the capital and its leader.

'It was a very dark night,' Sami starts tamely, with Huma adding, 'As usual.'

'No, actually,' Sami insists. 'It was the type that spies choose for a border crossing. I was in Military Intelligence then, not in ISI. The two of us, me and my junior, Murshid, caught him near the border in Sialkot sector after following him for half an hour. All three of us were very young then.' His eyes are distant, looking far away and long ago.

Huma inches forward on the sofa, her knuckles tense and eyes expectant. 'He had a gun?'

'No. Patience, girl!' Sami has a plan for his storytelling, a linear plan, one thing leading to another, no going back and forth like a wonky time machine. He has to watch out for the kids pulling him in all directions. Huma puts on her glasses as if she is watching a movie rather than listening to a story, 'You had guns?'

Sami refuses to get exasperated. Storytelling requires a cool mind, 'Of course we had guns. We were on border patrol, weren't we? And what is this about guns? You are watching too many *Alpha Bravos*.'

Sami has a strong urge to smoke but knows that Aalia would have none of it. 'So we had been following him, when dear Huma interrupted us,' he says somewhat testily. 'In fact, we were already a bit on the Indian side by the time we caught up with him, but he did not seem to know it. He said he had strayed into Pakistan by mistake. We quickly checked his clothes for labels. The labels were Indian. He said his name was Gopal Punjabi. He lived in a village nearby. We believed him. At that time we did not know that it was a very unlikely name for a Punjabi Hindu; that was pointed out years later by Ayesha, the clerk in the archives. "It's not a Punjabi name at all, except," she said, "as an adopted name taken by nostalgic Punjabis living in godforsaken places far away, the name being handed down the generations."

'Soon he would have realized that we were on their side of the border…and even the comatose Indian patrol couldn't have kept sleeping forever. So we left him and crossed back to our side. Next thing we know, we'd stumbled upon an abandoned well in a grove of trees, with a rusted iron ladder going down into it. There were fresh shoe prints on the parapet. Murshid goes down gingerly, while I shine the light from above. He is back in less than five minutes, with a plastic bag full of clothes stitched by a Sialkot tailor and an expired student ID card of Sind Arts College, Karachi. The ID card has a Muslim name and the photo of a smiling Gopal Punjabi.

'Both of us sat on the parapet and cursed ourselves. Here was an Indian spy who had obviously spent a lot of time in Pakistan under a Pakistani identity and we had caught him and then escorted him safely back to India! We had clear visions of being arrested, accused of being on the Indian payroll, tortured and shot. You see, we were in MI which theoretically may be at par with ISI, but in reality is a minion. It was too serious a matter for us to have kept quiet, either. Particularly when there were two of us and one could not have trusted the other not to squeal. When you are in the intelligence business, trust is a luxury you cannot afford.'

'So there we stood, outside a Brigadier's camp office in Naushehra, with the stupid plastic bag. Within two hours, a taxi with Sialkot numbers brought a man from ISI by the name of Colonel Imtiaz Gul, who actually looked like a portly property agent. He listened to us and between gulps from a water bottle, calmly informed us that if we mentioned the incident to anybody, we would meet a fate reserved for Indian spies.

'The threat did not surprise us at all. But what he said after that, did. Handing the package back, he ordered us to wait for nightfall, go back to the border and put it back in exactly the same place where we had found it. Only we could do this, he said, since only we knew where we had found it. "And after that, if you ever go in that direction again, I will personally put you through the wringer and have the leftovers posted to North Waziristan!"'

Aalia places two glasses of milk on the table, glares disapprovingly at Sami, mutters 'language' and goes back to the kitchen, shaking her head. From the window, they hear the rolling thunder of shutters being pulled down and secured, each followed by a round of barking by the street dogs. A car alarm goes off somewhere and a fire engine trundles through the bazaar, its gongs receding slowly in the distance. Huma and Saqib finish their milk in long gulps, eager to enter that long-ago world again.

'A week later, something wonderful happened to me. The Military Intelligence sent me on permanent deputation to ISI. I had been specifically asked for by them, I was told.

'And there I was, sitting in a waiting area on the top floor of the ISI headquarters, smarting from the strip searches downstairs. After an hour's wait, I was led through a maze of corridors and down a long staircase to a lounge, where two men were having coffee and sharing a joke—I could hear the laughter from outside. One was Col. Imtiaz Gul and the other when he turned towards the door, was Gopal Punjabi.'

Huma goes 'Ya Allah!' and starts spluttering. Saqib swallows the gum he has been chewing and complains, 'You should warn us.' Sami tries to suppress a giggle, making his paunch quiver like jelly. Thus rewarded, he resumes his story, promising himself to be as truthful to the kids as possible.

'That day I was inducted into ISI and sent for six months' training to Kabul. When I came back, I was given the charge of handling Gopal Punjabi, who, meanwhile, had been across the border one more time. Sitting at the corner table of the canteen one evening when most people had gone home, the Indian told me over several cups of tea and then dinner about his strange story.

'Tell us about his looks,' Huma prompts, thinking of herself as an aspiring writer.

'Well, we were of the same height, but he was athletic, had a sharp pencil moustache and a good sense of humour. Women in the admin liked him.'

'And the weather?' Huma persists.

'Why is weather important? We were indoors, weren't we?' Sami says irritably. 'Well, it was raining heavily, if you must know. One of those autumn showers, after which the chill deepens suddenly.

'My story from here on comes from what was in the dossier, from what he told me that evening and from what I saw myself as his supervisor over the next year or so till he earned his spurs and was on his own. But the three streams of information have merged in my mind since then and I can no longer tell which bit came from where.' Smiling playfully, he adds, 'And some of it I might just have made up. Making a gripping story out of plain reality—even spy reality—is not an easy job, me being no writer.'

'His name in the file was "Gopal Punjabi", to answer your earlier question, Huma, but nobody believed or cared about that part. Other entries in the dossier were that he was the only child of devout Hindu parents who were killed during Partition. He was eleven when he reached a village near Gurdaspur in India, just across the border, holding the finger of a distant uncle who brought him up. The village was so near the border that kites from Pakistan flew over it during Basant. Many of the entries in the dossier were written as bullet points, without any explanation. He was the only one in the school who took Urdu as the second language. He said that his father was a Urdu teacher and he wanted to keep an association of sorts with him. After finishing school, he ran away from home one night when the uncle hit him for being late in chopping fodder for the buffalo.

'So terrified was he of his uncle that he kept running, and half an hour later, found himself in Pakistan. He worked

at a confectionery shop in Lahore for six months, giving
a Muslim name and a Pindi address. He would sleep in
the shop, and whenever free, would romp around and play
street cricket with boys who worked at other shops. He
knew that sooner or later he would be found out. Besides,
he wanted to go to college. By the time his employer came
to the shop one day, Gopal was already back in his village
with five thousand rupees—which he had not stolen, as
you might think. Even as a boy, he was as honest as they
come. An old man near the border paid him the money in
Indian rupees for carrying a shoebox full of opium, which
he delivered to a woman waiting on the other side.

'Gopal made peace with his uncle. The money helped
and so did his persistence and hard work in the college
at Gurdaspur. There was nothing much about those
years in the file except that he graduated with a first-
class degree four years later. Whether it was a regular
practice for the Intelligence Bureau to tour the colleges
along the border for talent scouting is not known, but
according to Gopal, a couple of officers visited the area
and enlisted him. His proficiency in reading and writing
Urdu came handy.

'He was given basic training for two weeks in Delhi and
for one year with the 4th Kumaon regiment at Baramullah
in Indian-occupied Kashmir. These specifics were marked
as "Verified" in red ink in the dossier, with detailed
footnotes at the bottom.'

The humdrum noises from the street have quietened
down and, apart from the sound of an odd motorcycle

echoing off the walls of the narrow lane, all is quiet. Downtown Pindi is winding up for the day.

'His first posting was as a stenographer to the cultural attaché at the Indian High Commission in Pakistan, which had just shifted from Karachi to Rawalpindi, while Islamabad was still a work in progress. In April '65, a battle had broken out between Indian and Pakistani positions in the Rann of Kutch and Pakistan had made spectacular advances. Jubilations erupted at both the Army and ISI headquarters. There was this new-found confidence—they could push Indians back anywhere, anytime. A plan was made to infiltrate thousands of commandos into Kashmir. This eventually did happen, and led to a full-fledged war, but the exact dates and maps somehow reached the Indian army well in time.

'Suresh Raina, which was the name on his passport then, was suspected to have been single-handedly responsible for the information. The Indians whisked him away overnight to their embassy in Nepal, just before he could be caught red-handed. In Nepal, in just three months, he blew the covers of all ten ISI men posted there. He had purchased the information in Rawalpindi from a typist working in the ISI headquarters, and about to retire. He simply took a chalk and wrote the ten names, cover identities and Kathmandu phone numbers on the wall of the Pashupatinath temple. A reporter from a pro-India newspaper did the rest.

'For the next year, he was the IB man in Amritsar, sharing an office with the local police on Mall Road. He had appropriated for himself another makeshift office in the mental hospital, where he interrogated all the Indians returned by Pakistan, many of whom were mentally ill. Mentally challenged persons from both sides routinely stray across the border and land in jails. His job was to receive the returning mentally ill and verify their Indian antecedents and also to make sure that those who were normal had not been "turned around" to work for Pakistan. He would be present, often alone, at Wagah, standing next to a mental hospital van, quarrelling with relatives who had come to receive their wards. The doctors hated him, which was a pity because they could have made his work easier. But our Gopal Punjabi was an arrogant man and preferred to work alone, as we found out later.'

Aalia joins Huma and Saqib on the sofa. Though she's been hard at work in the kitchen, her fingers still continue to move nimbly at crochet work.

'It was at Wagah that Gopal met Naina, a stage artist of sorts, who worked in a rag-tag group that performed at weddings. Naina, whose real name was Jasjeet Kaur, used to come to Wagah from Amritsar on her scooter to pick up her father, who was a clerk in the Border Security Force. The two got married a month later. Gopal had just one condition: that she stop performing on stage. She had reluctantly agreed. The only people who attended the ceremony from Gopal's side were the two police officers who shared his office; his uncle had passed away the year before.

'Six months after the marriage, Gopal slipped across the border to meet an informer he had cultivated during his Suresh Raina days. Ten minutes into Pakistan and he was apprehended by the Rangers. Gopal had seen so many people with mental illness in the last year that it came naturally to him to act as one. The officer to whom he was brought had a mentally ill son who had walked into India one night two years before, but the Indians had sent him back. He kept Gopal in a cell for two days and then, to return the favour, told his assistant to push him back into India at night.

'Gopal's world had turned topsy-turvy in those two days. The police officers, his chums till a day ago, turned hostile and refused him entry to the office. When he tried to call the IB office in Delhi, the highest he could reach was the PA to the Deputy Director, who said he was not authorized to talk in specific terms, but if, hypothetically, a spy were to be caught in another country because of his independent action, the government would wash its hands off the man. It was written in the contract, he said, no claims, no pension. Gopal's detention by the Rangers had become known to Delhi. To make things worse, he had not sought permission before going into Pakistan, ironically for fear of leakages in the head office. When he insisted that his cover was actually quite intact and that nobody across the border recognized him as Suresh Raina, the person at the other end had asked, "Suresh who?" and disconnected.

'By the time he reached home, it was dark. Naina was out. It seemed she had tried on several dresses before going out. The room was strewn with them and reeked of cheap perfume. He made a few phone calls, with no results.

Demented with anger, he drove around the nearby villages and found her belly dancing at a wedding two hundred yards from the Pakistan border. Gopal came away quietly and stood in a shadowed patch near the road. He'd stolen a jute rope from a farm and tied it to a tree. He waited patiently on the other side. Some cars and a motorcycle passed. And then he saw Naina in her garish costume, complete with a pink headband and a round cap, on her scooter. Gopal closed his eyes, pulled the string and held it taut…

'Gopal Punjabi did not go home that night. He came to Pakistan, crossing in from the Samba sector, and was arrested. He said he was an Indian spy and wanted to see an officer from ISI. When asked for the reason of his defection by Col. Gul, he said that Pakistan was where he had spent the only years of love and happiness he had known. He also said that he was an exceptionally good professional and would be value for money for the ISI. He said he was done with patriotism. Col. Gul understood. It was a spurned man talking, spurned during the course of a single day by his country and by the woman he loved. For a man it adds up to rejection by God.'

Aalia looks at the children and then at Sami, 'Look at them. Both mesmerized. Who would say that they have classes early in the morning? And you, janaab, do the rest of dastangoi tomorrow. Take your pills and sleep.' After the children reluctantly pull themselves away from the room, she continues, 'Don't you have any sense of what should be told to children—"held the string taut" and all! Can't you skip some of the horrid details or change them to something like firing a gun? It won't alter the story, would it?'

'But this is the way it happened and they see much worse in Indian movies,' Sami says, with such simplicity that Aalia gives up.

~

The next day after dinner, with the *Alpha Bravo* and milk ritual over, the children ready and waiting and Aalia hanging on to every word from the kitchen, Sami resumes.

'The ISI is a hard-nosed organization. They value professionalism. And using an Indian spy against India has its own pleasures. They happily took him in. Absorbing a high-profile Indian spy was a challenge, but fortunately no photograph of Suresh Raina had ever been in circulation. The only limitation was that he could not be posted in Delhi where he might have been recognized.

Huma interrupts, 'So, he had already been recruited when you and Murshid caught him.'

'Yes, you are right.' For once, Sami does not mind the interruption.

'Col. Imtiaz Gul, his handler for the first six months and the only person who knew his real identity (other than the men on the top floor, I presume), recalled that the previous year, while the Rasool barrage was being built, a boat full of labourers, all young men from Sind, had capsized in the swirling Jhelum. There were no survivors, and no bodies had been found. Col. Gul procured the birth certificate of one of the dead men, and by the time he was finished, Gopal Punjabi's curriculum vitae read something like this: *Abdul Malik* (though that was not the name). *Born in 1936 at Sukkur, went to school there, joined Sind Arts College in Karachi, graduated with a first division. Passed the entrance examination and the interview held by the Federal Commission. Joined ISI seven years earlier, through the civilian stream. Two years training with MI, one year training with the CIA at Langley* (both of us, me and Gopal, actually went to America, but just for a month). *Deputed to ISI. Number two ISI operative in Kathmandu and Kuala Lumpur for one year each.* Every particular was stoutly backed up by records in each of these establishments, starting with the school.

'The defection of Gopal Punjabi became a legend in Pakistan, but nothing was publicly known about his Pakistani identity, not even within the agency. Otherwise, he would not have been able to work the miracles that he pulled off over the next five years. Miracles that the ulema of our country attributed to his having embraced Islam. His story even found its way into the curriculum of many madrassas. He was responsible for the killings of twelve RAW operatives in Ankara, Kuwait and Kandhar.'

Sami pauses to explain to the children, 'RAW is India's ISI.'

'Yes, we know. Abbu told us,' eight-year-old Saqib replies.

'He brought us the plans for the Pokhran atomic tests, three years ahead of schedule, which pushed Pakistan to put its own plans for the Kahuta Research Laboratory on a fast track...nuclear parity being restored in the long run between the two countries is owed largely to that early start.

Far too many things had happened, Sami thinks, all of which were important. Which ones to tell and which ones to let go? Some were far too gory. Some would bring back memories which he himself would prefer to keep safely interred. The children had school in the morning. He had to lead the Friday morning prayer, as the Imam was still unwell. Then he remembers that Gopal Punjabi is still alive in his story and he proceeds to rectify that.

'Four years after the country split up, after our humiliating defeat at the hands of Indian Army in East Pakistan, our generals were desperate to regain some prestige. Gopal Punjabi led twenty of our best men to Bangladesh. Their assignment was to stoke mutiny in an already restless army. The coup which resulted slaughtered Mujibur Rehman and his family, but in the chaos that followed, we lost many of our own men. One was Gopal Punjabi. He was thirty-nine then.

'There is an unwritten rule that spies are not given gallantry awards, even posthumously. There are good reasons for that. Otherwise he would have certainly received Nishan-i-Haider. On my part, I am grateful to Allah–Talah that He granted me an opportunity to play a small part in the making of a legend. In fact, there are times when a handler learns more from his agent than the other way round. This was one such time...

'And now children, it is quite late. You have to get up early for school. Shabba Khair and sleep well.'

* * *

A year later, Aalia's mind has still not worked through the complicated web of grief that Sami had left her entangled in, that second night of storytelling.

Sami was a talkative man even while dying, although he was breathless and could only manage short sentences in the few minutes before the shrieking ambulance from Rawalpindi Heart Centre woke up the children. He died on the stretcher, while being carried down the steep stairs. But those few minutes were enough for him to tell her what he wanted to, leaving Aalia dumbfounded and devastated.

'I am Gopal Punjabi...' Aalia had initially thought he was delirious. But there was more. 'Nobody spurned me. Naina did not exist... Nobody fired me... I had resigned my job after Nepal. I was posted in Amritsar but never joined there... Those things looked good on the CV and provided a plausible motive for doing what I had been planning for years. Even while in school... That is why I took Urdu as the second language. I was the only one in the whole class. At that time, becoming a spy was nowhere in my mind. But going back, somehow, was.... As a child the only thing I wanted was to live in this house. That was the only home I knew. I had nothing there, in India...

'Men should not be put in a position where they have to choose between their Flag and their Home. If they were really free to choose, most would choose home as I did. Or so I think.

'I led the squad to Dhaka in 1975. I was the only one who came out alive. Nobody knew in the mayhem who lived and who died. We were not even supposed to be there to start with. Gopal Punjabi was getting to be known a little too much. ISI used the opportunity to bury him. Col. Gul provided me another identity—that of Samiullah Ahmed Pasha. He is the one you met. But Rehman and Zeba must never know.'

Flushed and sweating, Sami could not talk for a while. When he did, it was with difficulty. 'I was a good professional. I was paid by both sides and I delivered. Nobody owes me anything. I do not owe anybody anything. Except you.

'Forgive me if you can…although I don't know how you ever could. I do want you to know that I tried to be a good Muslim, just so that you would not feel cheated on that count at least.'

~

Aalia still cannot fathom how a young man could give up his country and his faith just to fulfil a childish wish to go back to where he had once been happy. Just to be able to live in the house where he was born and where his parents had been killed in front of his eyes. And just to be able to sit for long hours in front of the school he went to as a child.

She looks up at Sami's picture hanging above the mantlepiece. For a second, she could swear that she saw, on the clean-shaven upper lip, a thin pencil moustache. She smiles for the first time in a year.

There are sounds coming up the stairs. The children are back from school.

RULDA'S DISCHARGE

It had been thirty-four years since Rulda was last at a railway station. The trains were much longer and far cleaner. His escort, Anoop, was a twenty-year-old boy in jeans, who carried a Walkman hooked to wraparound earphones over his turban-covered ears. Anoop helped Rulda climb to the upper berth, where, strangely emptied of all emotions, he lay listlessly. A tin trunk, painted green with yellow flowers, lay at his feet. All that it had was a few clothes, a Japuji prayer book, a rosary and many medicines issued by the hospital pharmacy that morning on his discharge from the Mental Hospital, Amritsar.

Rulda had known for many years that his mother and his only sister had died during Partition. Just eighteen months ago, he'd learnt—from a distant acquaintance who'd actually come to visit a new patient in the hospital—that his sister's husband and their infant son had managed to reach Delhi in 1947, perched on top of a train till Amritsar. His informant had returned to Calcutta and forgotten about the conversation, until he'd run into Rulda's nephew, Ranjot, in a train about six months ago, and told him about Rulda. Ranjot had immediately come to Amritsar to meet

Rulda and, after talking to him for an hour, asked him if he would like to come to Delhi and live with his family.

Rulda had panicked. He'd initially refused, saying that after living in a mental hospital for forty years, he didn't think he was capable of living anywhere else. He'd cringed when his nephew hugged him before going. For many days he'd hardly talked and paced restlessly in the ward every night. He even told the occupational therapist that the man who claimed to be his nephew was an impostor.

Ranjot, whose father had died in the late '70s, owned a successful transport business. He had work in Amritsar and came to meet Rulda every two weeks. Rulda gradually became less awkward and even began looking forward to the visits. Finally, he had agreed to move to Delhi. After Ranjot had signed the papers last week, his young assistant, Anoop, had been sent to bring Rulda to Delhi.

It was not as if Rulda had never been out of the hospital all these years. Far from it. Over the last ten years, he had gone to the market every week as part of the shopping detail led by the Store in-charge. But, for the first time in forty years, he would not be going to sleep in a mental hospital at the end of the day.

Rulda did not feel anything in particular—happiness, unhappiness, insecurity or liberation. Perhaps staying in a hospital for a lifetime took away the cheer you were supposed to feel at leaving it. Maybe it was the illness which blunted the edge of his feelings. He had heard such things being discussed in the seminars where he had been presented as a 'case'. The nurses would translate anything he didn't follow for him.

But Rulda knew that this was not the full explanation. Only a week ago, he had caught a shopkeeper by the collar when he had refused to take back the five kilos of turmeric powder which Rulda had found to be adulterated. He had felt anger, an intense visceral anger, which had in fact surprised him. Maybe anger was the only emotion hospitals left you with.

As he sat cross-legged with a glass of tea in his cupped hands, the train crossed the Sutlej bridge. Rulda was angry at himself for not feeling exhilarated. He remembered Fattu, who would have chided him, 'How many people do you know Ruldia, who have lived in a mental hospital for forty years and then found a family, a real family of one's own relatives? None. It is a miracle. If I were you, I would be very happy and grateful to Khuda. You should be too.'

Rulda did not feel anything more after Fattu's imaginary sermon, but he did not see any harm in being grateful to God always for everything—for good and for bad and for not feeling anything about it too. It was already dark, anyway, time for his prayer. He took out the beads and the Japuji wrapped in a cloth, put on his reading glasses, picked up his turban from the shelf and put it back on his head.

As he leaned over to get the turban, he saw that the two Sikhs on the other lower berth looked drawn and anxious, with blanched faces. Anoop was standing in the aisle and telling somebody with a transistor radio in the next cabin, 'BBC, BBC.' They were saying something about Prime Minister Indira Gandhi being shot by her Sikh bodyguards. And riots. Rulda did not think that it concerned him. It was not 1947 after all. It was 1984.

By the time he'd finished his prayers, the train had stopped at a station. He craned his head and tried to read the board. Sonepat. There was a commotion on the platform and then heavy footfalls rang through the corridor as several policemen stormed the compartment. A very random check of the passengers' belongings ensued. Uniformed men went around tapping the suitcases with their sticks. A policeman stopped next to Rulda's berth. Dark eyes, in a face bulging out of the straps of a riot helmet, sized him up and he said, 'Do you have to go to Delhi? If it is not important, get down here. Weather is not right there, Sardarji. Mausam kharaab hai.'

Anoop came from the next cabin and angrily demanded, 'Of course it is important. We did not board the train for a lark, did we now? Are there floods in Delhi?' he asked sarcastically.

'Of sorts,' the policeman nodded. He shrugged, looked at Rulda again and went away.

A dreadful panic started to build up in Rulda's chest. His mind conjured up images: he was drowning in swirling waters, trying to catch his suitcase floating away from him. Then, suddenly, it was all real. The train entered a dark tunnel full of muddy water gushing in from the other side of the city and everything became dark. The grimy water was splashing against the window panes. It was rushing in from below the doors and pouring down from the lights in the roof, which were going off one by one with popping sounds. A bloated cow floated by his berth as he recoiled in horror. And then, fascinated, he saw himself: five years old, wearing brass rings in his ear lobes, being carried through waist-deep water on somebody's shoulders, somebody whose body odour was so familiar.

He heard the dark putrid waves lapping just below the upper berth. The only other sound was that of the train, a dull droning hum, as if the engine was trying to push through the monstrous mass of water. The struggle lasted for an hour or maybe a minute. Then the lights came on one by one, unhurriedly, as if waiting for their turn in an orderly queue. And with a loud whooshing sound like a giant whale breaching water, the train surfaced into a city of zillion lights and everything was dry and crisp like fresh paper.

It slowed down on a platform teeming with people waiting to board. Anoop held Rulda by the arm and carried his trunk in the other hand. The waiting crowd pushed forward, made impatient by the sight of the empty compartment filling up with people who had pushed harder. There was a surge and somebody, to make way for himself, wrenched Anoop's arm away with a jerk. Rulda fell.

When he got up, shakily, he could not see Anoop anywhere, even though the crowd had thinned. Uncertainly, he started walking along with the flow of the crowd. He crossed a pillar which bore the name of the railway station— Hazrat Nizamuddin. He kept walking, keeping an eye out all the time for Anoop, till he found himself outside the station. He stood looking around, perplexed. There was a lot of shouting. A crowd had collected in the middle of the parking lot, which was full of auto rickshaws.

It was the earphones that he saw first, trailing on the ground. Through a gap in the crowd, he saw Anoop, his body being fixed to the ground with blows from hockey sticks, by men whose faces he could not see because the crowd was shifting every moment, yet moving as one. The hockey sticks came down in unison, and a chant went up, 'Khoon ka badla khoon'. Through another momentary gap in the crowd, Rulda saw yellow flowers, his trunk, lying next to a motionless Anoop. The last time he had seen a man's head burst open like a watermelon was many years ago. The man had kept running with the crimson slices sprouting out of his neck; but that the doctors had said was him hallucinating.

Then there was the heavy smell of kerosene in the air and the ground lit up with fire. Rulda knew that this was no madness; this was what they called 'reality' at the seminars he was presented at. Somebody shouted, 'Another Sikh!'

Rulda could run, even in chappals. He patted his pocket. His money was safe. An auto rickshaw swerved near him, but the driver, on seeing him, tried to drive away. Rulda had already jumped in. The driver glanced back at him but decided to keep going rather than waste precious time in arguing. He drove fast, but Rulda could see several motorcycles laden with young boys carrying sticks and jerry cans, following them at a distance. The driver turned into a lane and stopped after a few minutes.

'If you don't get down, they will set me on fire first.' Rulda looked at the young boy in jeans, no older than Anoop. He was standing with folded hands and pleading with him, tears in his eyes, to get down from the auto. The sound of motorcycles approaching became louder. Rulda jumped out, left the road and ran into the dark. He ran for what seemed like hours on uneven ground with thistly shrubs everywhere, till he stumbled against a pile of bricks, lying next to a freshly dug grave. In the dark, he could make out the dim rows and rows of headstones. He walked on, the only sound being the rustle of dried leaves against marble, till an old building, a complete ruin, loomed up in the dark. Several doorways appeared, but turned out to be just arched alcoves etched into the hard wall. He kept walking around the building, looking for the actual door, passing a pillar with an inscription, 'Chausath Khamba' in Urdu. He could read it, but it meant nothing to him.

Rulda jumped as a snake quietly slithered across his path into the grass. He thought it had eyes too big for a snake, blazing red, like the marbles that he used to play with as a child. He found himself inside a deep hall which was full of dust and bird droppings. Dry leaves rushed along the floor with the wind. He heard music coming from somewhere near. It sounded like a qawwali. It scared him and soothed him at the same time. Then, intermingled with the qawwali's strains, he heard Anoop's wails. Rulda ran out, wanting to follow the snake, which he now believed had been sent to save him, into a lane full of people. Young lads pulled at his kurta, wanting him to buy jasmine and rose petals at bargain prices.

Two men on a motorcycle roared past him, the pillion rider holding a jerry can. Petrified, Rulda started running again. His legs were shaking as he found himself on a wide road full of lights, with traffic zipping past mere feet from where he stood. He stood tentatively at the edge of the traffic for a long time. A taxi slowed and stopped next to him. The driver rolled down the window and asked him where he wanted to go.

Rulda asked, 'Is there a mental hospital in this city?'